DIVINE NATURE

JD ATKIN

Britain's Next
BESTSELLER

First published in 2016 by:
Britain's Next Bestseller
An imprint of Live It Publishing

27 Old Gloucester Road
London, United Kingdom.
WC1N 3AX

www.britainsnextbestseller.co.uk

Copyright © 2016 by JD Atkin

The moral right of JD Atkin to be identified as the author
of this work has been asserted by him in accordance with the
Copyright, Designs and Patents Act 1988.

All rights reserved.

Except as permitted under current legislation, no part of this
work may be photocopied, stored in a retrieval system,
published, performed in public, adapted, broadcast, transmitted,
recorded or reproduced in any form or by any means, without
the prior permission of the copyright owners.

All enquiries should be addressed to Britain's Next Bestseller.

Cover art by DreadedmanArt

Author photo by Future Chronicles

ISBN 978-1-910565-67-4

Printed in Poland

Acknowledgements

THIS book is dedicated to all that supported it from its infancy, to the legion of friends and strangers who decided to take a punt on the mad man in the hat and help drag it kicking and screaming into the realm of reality.

Of special mention is the Smiling Assassin whose constant attempts on my life keep me relatively sharp, the Sneinton Drinker's Guild who often provided safe harbour from the perils of over work and afternoon sobriety and, of course, the Parental Protocol Droids Alpha and Delta for without their support I would likely be more useless and ridiculous than I already am.

My infinite thanks go to Game Sandwich and DreadedmanArt (see the promotional video and cover art respectively) for pandering to my unreasonable and last minute requests for creative perfection and to my Editorius Maximus Supreme Charlotte who, through lack of sleep and with endless patience, managed to wrangle this whole fiasco into the novel you now hold in your hands.

Finally I dedicate this book to you, dear reader, for picking it up off the shelf and sticking with me this far.

You sound brilliant, fancy a pint?

Divine Nature

"Life, uh, finds a way." – Jeff Goldblum, Jurassic Park

–::–

"Killed by Death" – Lemmy Kilmister, Motorhead

–::–

Be partakers of the divine nature. […]Giving all diligence, add to your faith virtue; and to virtue knowledge; and to knowledge temperance; and to temperance patience; and to patience godliness; and to godliness brotherly kindness; and to brotherly kindness charity. I have inherited divine qualities, which I will strive to develop. – 2 Peter 1:4–7.

–::–

DATA TRANSCRIBED FROM THE VIDI-LOG OF:
Captain Horatio Scara

DATA RETRIEVED FROM [CLASSIFIED], STATUS: NON-OPERATIONAL

DATA RETRIEVAL DATE: [CLASSIFIED]

The zep' arrives at 07:30, though I can almost hear its low thrum.

The news broke this morning, and the men of the Ninth have been congratulating me ever since. Each journey through camp is weighed down by handshakes, back slaps and well wishes. I am jovial, I smile and nod and share stories, yet it is little more than an act to keep up morale.

I protested to Central Command, to Gladstone directly.

To be assigned such a position at this time, however prestigious, is madness. My years upon the battlefield are far from over. I am in my prime; I still hunger for battle and the spoils of victory. And it cannot be denied that my reputation as an accomplished Captain dampens the spirits of our foes, whilst buoying those of our own men.

Captain Horatio Scara, Captain of the Ninth, vicious bastard.

The effort in this sector needs me - despite our victories in the field, our enemies still hound us at every turn. Every district is a nest of vipers; guerrillas fighting in the broken streets while their commanders seethe and plot in the shadows. They are a bloody hydra of vast numbers and fanatical beliefs, a worthy foe for our superior tech and discipline.

My protests were dismissed. The decision has been made: Ventilus will be promoted to take my place. He is competent and accomplished, but uncreative. I wish him luck, though he will need far more than that if he is to survive in this place.

We lost the Marseilles this morning; she was overrun. They died in their hundreds, her guns firing until the last. That's all the war is now, nothing but carnage and madness.

The bastards.

If they would capitulate to reason, this war would be over within days. Hell, if they had yielded to reason in the first place, this war would have never started and the Earth would be mildly less wretched.

Though such thoughts are pointless now, eh?

Perhaps these lunatics serve a purpose? The idea has been discussed more than once in the mess.

The cynic would argue, that with the planet a dustbowl and the sea reduced to toxic mire, the war simply serves to speed up the inevitable extinction of humanity. Is it not a better death to be taken by the bullet, than to starve in the dirt? Is it not more valiant to fall in battle, than die choking on air turned black by soot and ash?

For now, it seems that I shall have neither.

My new appointment awaits; Commander of the Security Corps of the Institute. It's a wordy title for what is nothing more than a glorified warden.

It is an insult!

That fabled mausoleum, that ancient hive of quacks, that siphon of funds and resources that leaves our front lines scrabbling like rats for provisions. Every day of my life, we have been told that they hold the key to our salvation. Within their walls they work to end this war, to restore the Earth to Eden.

Bollocks.

There is nothing that will stop this war. No super weapon, no claptrap device, no nurtured maiden.

They are fools within their castle; picking and prodding, delivering false promises, sermonising while we fight and die to keep their pampered arses fat and comfortable.

And soon, I will have the honour of keeping them safe in their luxury.

The men congratulate me, though I leave them here to die.

Tonight, I shall sleep little.

Chapter One

THERE was smoke on the water, fire in the lower corridors.

The gunfire had sputtered to a halt just over two Changes ago, though the pained moans of the dying lingered a little longer. Man and machine blackened beneath bouquets of bright petals, twisting and crumbling as they fed the flames that flourished upon them. Butterflies of ash leapt from the fires, fluttering into drunken swarms that twisted through the halls.

A section away from the battlefield, Meris enjoyed the way the waves lapped against the smooth sides of the glass canal as she stretched her legs out over the gentle current. A cradle of thick metal cables, spotted by clutches of algae and rust, secured the canal to the smoke-stained ceiling. She arched her back, her fingertips just brushing the damp plaster ceiling that loomed above. It cracked at her touch, sending broken flakes tumbling into the empty hall below.

Her attention turned back to the water, her reflection dancing across the surface. The hanging canal was just one of thousands of similar glass waterways that threaded through the Institute like silver veins in a concrete beast.

Meris looped a slender arm around the nearest support, reclining against a cable pulled taut by the weight of the magnificent construct of water and glass. Despite the precarious position upon her pellucid perch, Meris felt no fear of the massive expanse that opened up beneath her. The vast, rubble-strewn hall, a tomb of long dormant devices and silent screens, was of little interest to the girl.

She leaned over her knees, causing the thin green tunic she had awoken in to shift against her skin. Her toes skimmed across the water, delighting in the sensation.

It was cool. Or was it?

She slipped in further, joy glinting in her violet eyes as the water twirled about her calves. Her brows knitted. Temperature was one of the many things she didn't really understand yet. It was fizzy, and silky, and sometimes popped. She had decided it was a peculiar thing.

She scrunched her face, an unpleasant memory flushing on her cheeks. Temperature may be strange at times, but not when it got angry; not when it became fire. Fire was horrid. Fire stung. Meris frowned at the pink burn that sulked between her thumb and forefinger. It was there this Change, but it wasn't always. She shrugged; it came and it went, another funny old thing.

A large fish glided by, its spade-shaped fins paddling lazily at the water. The plate glass channels that nestled among the rafters contained a bustling ecosystem that thrived, unassisted, above the ruination below. The fish regarded the watching girl with swiveling blue eyes.

Meris leaned further forward, her turquoise hair spreading across the water's surface like unfurling lily leaves. She smiled and waved, 'Hi, Fish!' It frowned, as much as a fish can. Its wide mouth opened and closed rhythmically as it considered the slip of a girl who called to it. The frown graduated into a scowl, a valiant effort on its part. The fish arced away; flashing a mottled pattern of brown and gold.

'Oh...' She waved once more as it disappeared through the rust-marred portal that separated this section of the canal from the next room, 'bye fish.'

Her attention quickly turned to a colony of red and white shrimp, that bustled amid a thatch of russet weeds. Meris observed quietly, her chin resting on the backs of her hands, hoping for an invitation to join in their activities.

The shrimp remained focused on their work, their filter-tipped legs snatching hungrily at invisible motes of food that tumbled through the current. They had no time for the girl who watched them, her heart-shaped face painted with mild melancholy.

Meris sighed, boredom and solitude rumbling through her mind. Her gaze returned to the water's rippling surface, where broken shards of her reflection stared back at her. Meris's eyes narrowed, pouting in mock irritation.

On command, a pointed flower bloomed at her temple. The long, fuchsia petals dashed with the brightest of white speckles teased a slow smile from her reluctant lips. She closed her eyes; willing one, two, three more into being, delighting as they pushed through her hair to frame her face.

Leaves, too! At her thought a flurry of leaves, green and hungry, rushed from her skin. She shivered with excitement as they danced across her shoulders in all shapes and sizes; long and thin, broad and strong, more and more bursting from the nape of her neck and racing down her spine.

Her thin gown melted away before their march. What little warmth it had provided was replaced tenfold as the leaves opened, devouring the simulated daylight that strained from hundreds of hissing monitors set high on the surrounding walls.

Meris buzzed with childish glee. She wiped a film of ash and dust from the glass, creating a mirror in which a bouquet grinned and pulled faces. She giggled, drawing the halo of petals down her cheeks to spread across her neck and chest. The rustling of leaves rose above the constant babbling of the waterway as the botanical battalion fought to occupy any area of exposed skin.

She turned her head this way and that, enraptured by her own reflection as she slowly became more plant than girl. Her moss-covered hands touched upon her face, her mouth agape as tiny green tendrils wormed from her fingertips. More plant than girl - would that be so bad? Her leaves bobbed with encouragement as she pondered upon this notion.

Meris the Plant twisted around herself. Lifting one knee from the water, she drew it to her breast, her eyes resting on three smaller flowers blooming from a nest of diamond-shaped leaves on her wrist. Snapping roots chased tiny rivulets of water as they trickled down her ankle and seeped out across the glass wall of the canal. The fleeing droplets slowed as they soaked up the dust, each one creating a channel for the next to surge along. The first soon reached the edge of the canal frame, and dithered a moment. Dim light spiralled within it as it trembled at the brink, before descending the crystal wall and diving towards the desolate floor some two hundred feet below.

More plant than girl, hmm? She swished her leg through the water, rousing groans of protest from the nearby shrimp who twitched their feelers angrily at the rush of displaced water. She retracted her leaves long enough to make an apologetic expression, and withdrew from the water. Already she could feel a slight strain weigh upon her; an addiction gnawing at her mind, tempting her to return to the safety and support of the Network.

She hugged her legs tighter. She didn't often leave its nurturing embrace, and the sensation of being removed from the water was an odd one. Since she had awoken there had been little opportunity and even less reason to venture from the streams. The world beyond was hard and dry, filled with sharp edges that prodded, poked and bit into her skin.

Meris shed a few more leaves, exposing her forearm, and watched as her flesh began to harden. The pale, almost-translucent skin took on a deeper colour, thickening automatically to provide her some protection from the world at large. Maybe her flowers would prefer it out here? They needed the water, but equally so the land, the fresh air.

The creatures of the canals - the brilliant fish, and scuttling crustaceans - didn't much care for her flowers.

They preferred the corals, fussing about her when she slipped in amongst the reef, her body spreading into a mass of waving branches, bouncing polyps and dancing anemones. Corals were nice, she could not deny it. They were all fat and squishy, their gabbling voices ebbing and flowing as they sang their silent songs in the nutrient-rich waters. Still, in her heart, Meris couldn't help but secretly admit that the flowers held her heart.

Flowers loved the air, and yearned for the sun even more than her corals did. Green leaves drank in light that was pure and free, without the undulating filters the water created. Despite herself, she dropped her leg back into the water, swishing it again and feeling guilty for doing so.

The fish may not like her flowers, but she was sure other creatures would. Creatures like the bees.

Bees! She gasped aloud, her hands flying to her face with more than a hint of theatrics. The sound echoed through the room, returning from the far walls like the whispers of an autumn wind. She wondered and worried about bees. She knew *of* them, calling their image to her mind's eye from some distant place; a stranger's memory. She closed her eyes. Dainty feet and shimmering wings, twirling tongues and oval eyes filled with the warmth of summer evenings.

Beneath the curling petals, Meris's face contorted with concentration. Her breath pooled, held in her breast, her fingers gripping the palms of her hands as she wished, she willed for bees.

Fuzzy, buzzy honey bees.Chubby, woolly bumblebees. Humming bees, thrumming bees, yes please!

The vegetation that swaddled her in layers of petals and leaves bloomed in greater bursts than ever before. Her small body shuddered as branches erupted from her back, stretching through the air as ever more foliage exploded from their tips. Vivid green vines dripped from her like honey, creeping across the glass and dropping flat round leaves and yellow lilies into the water.

She exhaled slowly, a long continuous breath that seemed to go on forever. Her eyes fluttered open tentatively, barely hiding the bright excitement that swelled within them. "Bees?" she asked in a small voice, peering from within the cluster of emerald flora that enveloped her. "Helloooo..." she called, daring to raise her voice just a little. "Hello, bees?"

Only the faintest crackle of distant gunfire, and the ever present babbling of water responded to her. The movements of the plants that grew from her ceased, the vegetation frozen in expectation. "Hello?" she called again in a shrill voice, high with defiant hope.

Once more, the high walls sent her voice echoing back to her. Of the buzzing and bumbling of bees there was none. She sighed in abject disappointment. A slump weighed upon her shoulders, whilst the flowers that bloomed about her face wilted dejectedly.

Why couldn't she make bees?

"Why can't I make bees?" she cried aloud, scowling at the echoes that mocked her.

She had tried to make bees before, she was certain. Somewhere long forgotten, she had tried and failed. She winced - though she didn't know why - as a branch receded into her shoulder blade, crunching as it collapsed back into her body. She could 'turn off' pain sometimes; it ebbed and flowed, just another strange thing.

Petals fell from her like gentle snowflakes, landing in the water and drifting downstream in ones and twos. Her leg dipped sulkily back into the water, as her body sloughed the vegetation's verdant grasp. Castoff leaves spiralled downwards, decaying in mid-air, to bolster the endless drifts of dust below.

Her eyes glared upwards, the alien stain of anger wrought upon her angelic features. "Why?" she cried at the vast portrait of herself that dominated the hall's distant, smoke-blackened wall. Fresh tears stung her eyes, the repeated question choking her. "Why can't I make bees?!"

Her own face stared down from the ancient propaganda, an expression of stern benevolence fixed across her face. "I bet *you* could make bees," she whispered moodily, her gaze turning inwards, "I bet *you* could do anything." Tears defied her rage to splash quietly into the running water, shimmering as they held their form beneath the gentle waves. She swayed her legs pensively, scowling accusingly at them. The long-forgotten shrimp had fled at her earlier outburst, and now she sat alone.

There was a click, and a hum. The subtle susurration that leaked from the screens shifted pitch. Meris lifted heavy eyes, pink tinted, gazing up to where pixels danced on electric displays. The whites and blues that had previously simulated the summer sky gave way to an autumnal palette of oranges and reds, as the artificial sun began to set.

Above her, the portrait gazed out into the hall. The twilight emphasised her severe beauty, highlighting her in defiance of the shadows that crept across the walls. Meris yawned. The green tunic had returned and now thickened as she pulled it about her slender frame, shrouding her from the gathering darkness. Where it touched the water Meris's skin glowed like distant moonlight. A smattering of small bewhiskered fish flitted past, scavenging along the base of the canal, their pale scales winking in the shades of sunset. Meris watched them disappear, rushing away into the growing gloom. Hidden amongst the eaves as the dusk closed in around her, she nuzzled against the rough side of a twist of cables, barely feeling the pitted metal against her skin.

With one last click and a final hum, darkness fell, and the Change was done.

Synthetic night fell upon the Institute. From the shadows the portrait glared at the world, its eyes burning with detached joy.

DATA TRANSCRIBED FROM THE VIDI-LOG OF:
Captain Horatio Scara

DATA RETRIEVED FROM [CLASSIFIED], STATUS: NON-OPERATIONAL

DATA RETRIEVAL DATE: [CLASSIFIED]

I've been here for three weeks. Three long, stinking weeks I have walked these decrepit halls and watched over its sheltered inhabitants.

The stories of opulence and luxury are no more than wishful speculation. The Institute is a museum, a relic, a dump.

Nothing works. What power we have comes in fits and starts, from a rheumatic power array that must be centuries old. The comms systems are patchy at best, and the automated defence network - if it's even operational - is in painful need of an upgrade.

My team of division leaders - an oddball mix of grizzled veterans and inexperienced greenhorns with powerful fathers - have been vital in developing my understanding of this place, though what is fact and what is rumour is hard to distinguish.

I have made multiple requests to meet with the Master of Engineers to address these issues, but thus far he has proven to be elusive.

Unfortunately, Professor Cornum Porvine has not been so absent. The bloated old greybeard is the head of the Science Corps, the army of boffins in their blue lab coats that scurry around the place like mice within a vast cathedral. As such, he is the de-facto ruler of this little island, a position he is more than happy to fill. He is blustery, deranged and held in a level of high esteem I find completely unfathomable.

He has also become my shadow. His reports, or requests for my input on some trivial matter, interrupt my duties on an almost-hourly basis.

I have made a game of trying to avoid him. In this place, it is not too hard. Its halls and corridors stretch on for miles, section after section of laboratories filling every tower and descending into every basement. Service halls, residential quarters and warehouses full of supplies jostle for space, and throughout the complex, the Network - the labyrinth of glass tubes and suspended canals teeming with all manner of aquatic life - extends across every level like a glass spiderweb.

The fish are, at least, pleasant to observe, and a fine distraction from Porvine's many sermons.

It appears that the work of the Science Corps has turned to the stuff of myths and legends. Their labours focus foolishly on the construction of the impossible.

"Engineered divinity," they call it; cellular bio-mechanics so advanced that it has become indistinguishable from works of sorcery. Porvine claims they are replicating the crucible of life itself, folding it into a sentient consciousness that they can control.

In lay terms: a man-made god, a clone of the Creator, dangerous nonsense.

These scientists have no idea what fire they have lit in the world outside these walls.

The Army of Agnostics, the Human League, the Consortium of United Atheists, the Church of Evolution and the Mother's Men in their red cloaks; thousands take to the streets in opposition of what they do here. Their numbers swell the ranks of our enemies; their anger spills the blood of good soldiers.

And for what? The age-addled dreams of some old men?

I have contacted Central Command. Gladstone should have

been made aware long ago of how these loons waste our time and money.

I have yet to receive a reply.

It pains me to rot in here, idly watching the fish while men die on distant battlefields, fighting to keep the wolves from our door. I will increase patrols in the compound both inside and out.

It will do well to keep the men active.

Chapter Two

A heavy blow fell upon the dark wooden doors that lurked in the corner of the hall, shattering the silence. A second strike smashed the lock, and sent grey dust flying from the intricately carved panels. An avalanche of harsh voices and orange firelight spilled through the widening gap, tearing into the tranquillity that previously filled the vaulted hall.

Meris woke with a start and a squeak. She moved quickly, dismissing the last lingering petals from her brow before sliding into the water, making no sound as she hid beneath the rippling surface. She held her human form for now, though made a conscious effort to reduce her natural bioluminescence.

Far below the doors struggled open, demolishing a drift of detritus that had slouched against them for countless years. The girl watched wide-eyed as two large men shouldered into the hall, dragging a third between them.

A hubbub of shadowed faces clustered behind the trio, each vying to follow them into the deserted room, but none brave enough to be the first across the threshold.

"Close the fuckin' door," the first barked, "and bar it, I want some fuckin' privacy with him. Besides, we don't want this slippery fucker getting any ideas now, do we?" He took hold of the captive firmly by the collar, and cast him bodily into the room. The unfortunate chap tried to remain standing but failed, his legs betraying

13

him and sending him sprawling across the marble floor. He groaned, blood dripping from his mouth to splatter across broken fingers that splayed out before him. He winced, his body battered and bruised, and forced himself to his knees.

The third of the trio set down his mean-looking rifle, propping it against an ornate balustrade. "Bar it?" he complained, tearing the red cloth mask from his face to reveal a roughly shaved head and a heavily scarred face. "Bar it with what?"

Number One turned from his prisoner, rubbing the back of his own balding head irritably. "Use your imagination," he scowled, gesticulating with his free hand. "And check the others as well, I don't want any surprises. And *you*..." he kicked at the kneeling captive with a hobnailed boot, raising another groan of pain. "Move!"

The two men descended the stone staircase, the suffering prisoner pausing only briefly and earning a vicious cuff to head for it, before stepping into the hall proper. Behind them, the third man - who we shall aptly name Number Three, for now - jammed his rifle across the curling door handles, barring it from the inside. Grumbling, he trudged across the room to where an identical pair of doors waited and pulled upon them. The locks held firm.

"We're good here Latt." he grinned, identifying Number One, "I've secured both doors!"

"So what do y'want, a fucking medal?" Latt sneered. "Get the fuck down here."

Number Three adopted a sour expression, and stuck his hands into the pockets of his grubby trousers. His muscle-clad form hunched moodily as he kicked at a piece of broken masonry, sending it bouncing down the steps. "Only fuckin' sayin'," he grumbled as he followed it down towards the two men.

Latt's attention turned back to the blue-coated man before him. He grinned cruelly, lifting him to his feet before shoving him forwards once again. "Nearly there Scara," he laughed, "nearly there." Their destination was a huge and ancient array of dust-clad computers and various techno-gubbins that rose in gradual steps to dominate the wall before them.

Cobwebs hung from the heights like tropical creepers upon a jungle pyramid, twisting around the minute blinking hieroglyphs that dotted its surface. A greedy rictus grin split Latt's face, a fissure of stained teeth dividing his heavy features from the sprawling beard of russet hair that held dominance over his square chin and thick neck.

The temple of technology acknowledged them with a beep as one man walked, and one man limped towards its sprawling lower levels. Another electric beep, both near and far away, answered the first. Motion sensors twitched and clicked like beetles, relaying the men's presence into the heart of the machine. Pipes rattled and shook, coughing great gouts of dust out into the room.

Latt clapped his hands together as a forest of mechanical arms extended like the myriad legs of an iron crab, whirring out from the upper echelons as they lowered a number of cracked and spotted screens down from the heavens. A few seconds passed as they slotted together, the machine adjusting itself here and there until they formed a single, gigantic display. A gang of keyboards crept out from the shadows to slide guiltily into position beneath it.

"Come on..." Latt muttered impatiently, cracking a knuckle. Behind him Number Three said nothing, standing in silent amazement.

The screen flared into life, crackling and hissing. More than one panel showed nothing but static. The computer shook each of them with synthetic irritation until at last conformity reigned, and a single word in pixelated letters six feet high hovered before them.

[KEY?] The venerable machine asked, flashing the word onscreen; its vocal interface having long-ago burnt out.

Scara regarded it ruefully, dugongs of despair swimming in the pools of his eyes. He lowered them to the floor, unwilling to look upon what awaited him.

"Come on then Scara, come on old mate," Latt said in a dangerously-chummy way, wrapping an equally chummy arm around his new friend's forlorn shoulders, "don't keep us waiting, eh? No need to keep us waiting, not now." The captive remained silent, his grey eyes fixed upon an indifferent crack in the tile at his feet. His blond locks, stained into heavy ropes by smoke and grease, hung from his temples.

He said nothing.

Latt's patience evaporated with record speed. He shook him, his meaty fingers crushing into Scara's shoulders, his voice growling in his throat, "The Key Scara, the fuckin' Key. Where is it?"

Scara said nothing. Fat droplets of blood slithered from his fresh wounds, crimson dancers cartwheeling through the air to their demise upon the grey stone. He had remained silent during his captivity; enduring the last three Changes, and weathering the vicious beatings dealt to him without a word. He would hold firm - his allegiance was sworn to Her, and with Her blessing he would find a way through this; he would find a way to hide the Key, or destroy it before they got their hands on it, unless death took him first.

He said nothing.

Then he smirked.

The blow, when it came, was as brutal as it was inevitable. Scara fell heavily against the lower steps, a choked cry betraying him. Pain gnawed at his chest; another broken rib. His collection was really growing.

The third man jogged down the staircase, regarding the groaning Scara with bristling eyebrows raised.

"You getting there, Latt?" He asked cheerfully, rocking on his heels and grinning broadly.

Latt scowled at him, "Does it look like I'm fuckin' getting anywhere, Lott? Is that what this looks like to you?" He presented Scara like a showman revealing his main attraction. Scara was otherwise occupied trying, and failing, to find the least painful route back to standing. Latt kicked him hard, sending him reeling back to square one. "Do I look like a man who has 'got there', huh? Does he look like he has given me the directions to anywhere remotely fuckin' close to 'there'?"

Lott, identified at last, shrugged. "S'pose not."

His brother's eyes narrowed, though he held his tongue, instead turning back to questioning the captive that groaned on the ground next to them.

"I won't fuckin' ask you again," he growled "now stop being a righteous prick and tell me where the fuckin' Key is!" Latt leaned against the balustrade, visibly exasperated by the protracted nature of the interrogation.

He loosened the thick, red scarf that coiled about his upper body; tugged at the woollen loops to allow some air to get to his pink neck.

"Look, Scara," he sighed, dripping transparent reason with every syllable. "It's over, it's done, isn't it?" Scara coughed, pushing himself to a sitting position.

His head remained bowed. He remained silent.

17

"Ok, you're a vicious fucker, I'll give you that." Latt continued, holding out his hands, palms up in a peaceful sort of way, "Your lot have fought well. Fuck me, you fought a lot harder than we expected when we finally got in here. But now... come on, even *you've* got to see that you've lost?"

He stood and walked towards the waiting computer screen, turning his back on his defeated foe and watching twin. He folded his arms behind his head, rocking thoughtfully upon his heels.

"Winners and losers, Scara. Winners and losers, it's always the way. Come on, give me the Key. I'll kill your pet abomination, or whatever it is you have in here, and then we'll be on our way." He flashed a sinister grin over his shoulder and clapped his hands together, "Simple as you like. Now be reasonable, give us the Key."

"Yeah, give us the key." Lott sneered, wanting to chuck his two pence in for what it was worth, and as he was also a mean spirited bastard, putting the boot in while he had the chance.

A pained croak rose from his victim as he doubled over in pain, clutching at his burning chest. Despite the pain, he stuck to his guns and remained silent vis-à-vis the location of their desired item. There was no way he was going to let them get to that Key.

"What the fuck, Lott?" Latt groaned, knuckling his forehead in exasperation. "What the fuck did you go and do that for?"

Lott shrugged, a self-satisfied grin slinking away to be relieved by a glum expression of weak justification, "I, I dunno." he shrugged, scuffing his heavy leather boot across the tile. "He was just pissin' me off, y'know."

Latt pinched the bridge of his nose and put a hand upon his brother's shoulder. The prisoner gurgled upon the floor.

"Well, if you wouldn't mind hangin' off laying into him while I'm in the middle of an interrogation, now that, that would be just fuckin' *brilliant*." He locked eyes with his sibling, one hand gripping his skull. "We have tried the violent approach haven't we?"

"Yeah, I guess." his brother mumbled.

"And that has not yielded very much now, has it?" the bearded one continued, "Has it?"

"No Latt, it hasn't." grumbled the admonished Lott, eyes down.

"No, it hasn't." Latt repeated, patting Lott's stubbly jowls.

Latt closed his eyes and sighed heavily, letting go of his twin to make placating gestures with his hands. Then in a single motion, he drew a heavy handgun from a leather holster at his side and turned it on the prisoner. "Now, Scara!" he roared, "Tell me where the fuckin' Key is, or I'm going to blast your brains all over this fuckin' building, comprende?"

DATA TRANSCRIBED FROM THE VIDI-LOG OF:
Captain Horatio Scara

**DATA RETRIEVED FROM [CLASSIFIED], STATUS:
NON-OPERATIONAL**

DATA RETRIEVAL DATE: [CLASSIFIED]

Still no word from Central Command or Gladstone's office.

I admit I am growing concerned.

The feeling of isolation has begun to affect me. The solitude this place exists in is unnatural, and has clearly had an effect on those who have been here for an extended period, though their productivity does not seem to have changed much. As I speak, the boffins are increasing their activity; there is talk of a breakthrough.

I ceased attending their tedious meetings several weeks ago, but may resume doing so - if only out of idle curiosity. I have instructed my men to keep an eye on all staff, and report anything they deem suspicious directly to me.

Communications are being monitored.

So far only one word has shown an increase in frequency: "MERIS".

I will speak with Porvine directly.

Chapter Three

MERIS watched, transfixed, from beneath the waves of her lofty hiding place. Though the conversation below was muted by the water, it was clear to the fascinated girl that something very bad was happening. Something very bad was always happening wherever humans were concerned; this was a lesson she had learned early on.

Eight or nine Changes had passed since she first awoke; floating within a billowing cradle of transparent tubes and torn wires that coiled and writhed like the silicon tentacles of a robotic jellyfish. The scars that marked where they had bored into her flesh returned from time to time; the pink ovals bubbling across her pale skin, their hues rippling as the faded memories returned to her in dribs and drabs.

She had drifted listlessly, lost and unknown amongst the flotsam that flowed through the vast network of suspended rivers. Beyond the glass, the world was a blur of darkness and ruin. The broken shapes of abandoned machines passed in the gloom, like the ghosts of great beasts. Lights glimmered in the distance, brilliant blue electric flares and the hungry reds of consuming fire. Alone she travelled through the Institute, descending from the barren upper levels and down into the bustling reefs.

She recalled the fish; the first fish, red and yellow fluttering above her half-blind eyes. The gentle current bore her through the iridescent shoals that swirled through the canals, exploding like living fireworks in smaller groups before rejoining their ever-changing ballet. Tiny mouths nibbled pleasantly at her skin, nuzzling and pushing against the transparent tubes that bound her. Like autumn leaves these fell one by one from her body, tumbling away until at last she was able to swim free.

And swim she did.

The girl melted and morphed, folding her previously-human form to swim as countless species of fish, in hundreds of different shoals. Beneath the gentle waves Meris chased and dove, raced and weaved amongst the other fish with unrestrained ichthian joy. She had immersed herself almost completely; not only in their delight and curiosity, but also in their shared fears. She fled and hid amongst the marine life, and watched with them as the humans waged their vicious war in the great halls, winding corridors and ruined laboratories of the Institute below. Red and Blue fought from floor to floor, while fire and blood painted grotesque murals across the walls.

In a thousand bodies she had wandered the Institute's endless grey purgatory. She had swum unseen through halls filled with gunfire and smoke; darkened rooms where blue-cloaked scientists worked furiously at humming computers, their faces tinged green by the glow of flickering monitors. She had seen blood spill from kneeling men, the violent crimson dashed across electronic altars. In vaulted cathedrals hydraulic machines stretched and fussed over rows of shadowy tubes that housed pale bodies, whilst far below twisted voices cried out their desperate prayers.

And above it all, watching every battle, every death and every desperate soul with those cold eyes was The Portrait. Her own face smiled down upon it all, serene and superior, forever cruelly detached from the world it observed. Meris hid from those eyes, from that inhuman smile, from those features that inspired such love and such hatred in the humans below.

She watched now, hovering in the gentle stream; her human form shimmering as she fought the temptation to shift, the temptation to hide. She should leave; of this, she was certain. She should dissolve into the living waters, to flow amongst the corals and away to a place of safety. But her human form - her arms and legs and hair and fingers and... and well, *everything* - these were precious and dear to her. Despite the fear that twinkled in her breast like a distant star, she was loathe to leave it even for a second.

She pressed a delicate hand against the glass, and watched the scene unfold.

"I'm not fuckin' around here, Scara." Latt forced him to stand, dragging him up by his hair. "I mean it Scara; tell me where the fuckin' Key is!" Latt's face was in turmoil, as reds and purples fought to become the dominant hue; the throbbing veins in his neck egged them on, and tried to surpass his eyes in the bulging championships.

Scara was thrown against a blinking bank of computer gadgetry as his captor repeated his demands. Defiance flared across his rugged features as his silence broke. "Fuck you, sweet cheeks!" he spat, forcing a pained grin across his swollen jaw.

Latt flicked his gun to the side and fired a shot, deafening Scara and punching a crater in a nearby wall. The impact rumbled about the hall, dislodging chunks of stained plaster that crumbled from the ceiling and splashed into the water beside the watching girl.

Lott smirked and wiggled a finger in his ear.

The ugly handgun made a satisfied click as another slug settled into place before swinging back to snarl at

Scara's chiselled, yet understandably dishevelled profile. Blood wept quietly from his closed eye, pushing a gentle course down through the bristles that clustered upon his cheeks. "Sorry Latt," he said with mock sincerity, "that was rather rude of me. What I meant to say was, 'I'm very sorry but I don't know what, or where this Key you are talking about could possibly be. Now kindly go and fuck that pretty little brother of yours, he looks lonely. There's a good boy." He managed a winning - if rather bloody - smile.

Meris lifted her head from beneath the waves, blinking diamonds of water from her eyes as she peered down into the gloom below. The man in blue; that face, that voice, she recalled something, a funny old something. Images swam in her mind, half-memories of blue coats behind walls of glass, distant voices and the feel of metal on skin, of needles in flesh, of fire.

Her fingers closed about the side of the glass channel as, despite the fear that tugged upon her, she drew herself out of the water. She craned over the side, desperate for a better view of the goings on below, for a better view of the man in blue. Rivulets of water slipped from her turquoise tresses and skipped across her skin, leaping like salmon to pepper the dry floor below.

The precipitation of curiosity went unnoticed by the trio, two of whom had become almost blinded by affronted rage. "You what!? You fuckin' what?" Lott barrelled forward, murder on his mind and spittle on his lips.

Latt, being the closer of the two, struck first. The barrel of his ungainly weapon crashed into the side of his captive's head, spraying blood and flinging him once again against the battered keyboard. Scara managed to stifle a cry this time, tiring of this ping-pong style of interrogation. "Cocky fucker!" bellowed Latt, jettisoning patience like a rage-fuelled rocket.

[INCORRECT INPUT – PLEASE ENTER KEY] flashed up on the flickering screen.

Latt turned his gun sideways and thrust it towards the recoiling man. Then, remembering he was not a young urban hoodlum, returned it to the correct position. "The Key, Scara. Gimme the Key or you fuckin' die!" There was a great deal of gun-thrusting.

Lott, his own gun still filling the role of makeshift lock, stood beside his brother, fuming in a rather volcanic sort of way. To say he was livid would be an understatement.

Meris's thoughts were a speeding zoetrope, her eyes glazed as streams of grey memories flickered across her mind. Her heart burned in her chest, thrumming wildly as she fought to grasp wriggling motes of meaning from the whirlwind of images in her head.

The man in blue was important; the man in blue was in pain. Did she say that aloud? Or that?

She clutched at her head, almost dislodging herself from her position amongst the arches. Something stirred inside her, a fizzing, racing something that rippled like lightning beneath her skin.

Things began to happen – well, two things, to be precise.

Meris watched, immobilised, as threads of glistening gold light flowed like electric honey through her veins, illuminating her from the inside out. Pain hit her then, and such pain it was! She reeled, her back arching, her muscles spasming as it raced through them. She clenched her jaw, suppressing a scream.

Teeth snatched at her, claws drove into her, and stingers pierced her skin. Agony ensnared her, consumed her, though it was not her own suffering, oh no. This was empathetic pain, misery siphoned directly from those around her. She could feel it keenly, as though she wore the wounds herself.

Her hands tightened into fists, determination hardening her features. This suffering... she could master it. She *would* master it. It snarled within her as she moved through it, her mind's eye opening.

The world before her became a saffron-hued fog, and at its heart lay the defiant agony of the Man in Blue, of Captain Horatio Scara, shining like a beacon that drew her forth. Her mind answered the call, absorbing his thoughts, his memories, words, pictures, data; knowledge seared itself into her consciousness.

Meris knew his name, she knew how he suffered, and she knew each of his broken bones as though they were hers, she felt his damaged flesh as though it clung to her own skeleton. She knew the pain of failure, of defeat, of betrayal. She knew, for the first time, what it was to be human.

Tears blossomed in her eyes. She must do something, she *must* help him. Meris breathed deeply, her mind searching for a connection, her body aflame with pulses of energy. She could do this! She was brave, and she *could* help him.

DATA TRANSCRIBED FROM THE VIDI-LOG OF:
Captain Horatio Scara

DATA RETRIEVED FROM [CLASSIFIED], STATUS: NON-OPERATIONAL

DATA RETRIEVAL DATE: [CLASSIFIED]

There has indeed been a breakthrough, though I am still sceptical that it will become something worthwhile.

Despite their quirks, and against my better judgement, over the months I have been posted here I have found myself warming to a number of my colleagues. Though my posting here prevents me from helping my comrades in the field - a fact that still wounds me deeply - I cannot help but harbour a secret hope that this gaggle of oddballs are on to something.

It is probably some form of Stockholm syndrome. I must be going mad.

Porvine made no secret of it. The construction of the MERIS had been their goal from the beginning.

The Institute feels more like a church than ever. The image of the stone woman that parts the waterfall in the main foyer now hangs upon great tapestries in every hall. The walls are plastered with her likeness, propaganda fliers with the Institute's words, 'Your future, Our Promise,' dripping all over them.

She is supposed to look carefree and welcoming, the words full of earnest. I find it oddly sinister, in a final sort of way. Perhaps I am going mad.

There is no wonder our enemies fight us so.

There is still no word from Central Command, or from Gladstone.

We intercepted a number of transmissions, though the signal was badly degraded. It appears we have achieved a number of decisive victories in the field. I admit, I still rue that I was not part of them. The Army of Agnostics have disbanded, and so too have the Human League. In addition, Command now has control of a number of districts previously held by the Church of Evolution.

The Mother's Men have reduced their guerrilla campaign, though remain an active presence. There have been scattered reports of defectors to their cause; I hope Command are able to nip this one in the bud. The Consortium of United Atheists still control a significant portion of the North and West, and so remain a considerable threat.

For now, we must continue to win their hearts and minds.

Our scouts report no activity on the island. The automated defences still remain inactive; the Master of Engineers has yet to be found, therefore a replacement will shortly be elected. My men have been ordered to double their training routine.

Though the chances of enemy action are low, we must be prepared for anything.

Chapter Four

SCARA'S left eye had swollen shut, his right glared monoptically down the barrel of Latt's brute of a handgun. He fought to remain standing as the man continued to shout at him. The blows and the gunshot had shattered his hearing, reducing a world of sound to a thrumming tintinnabulation.

He reached out a bloody hand, trying to steady himself against the angular mechanical array. His left side erupted into a shower of agony as his arm took his weight, each torn muscle and broken bone clamouring to make their protests heard. It was to be expected. Death was doubtless imminent. He must have seconds at best; this was the end.

Despite his poor physical condition, Scara found himself oddly at peace. Soon, the pain would subside and he would go to his death. It was a good death. He did his duty, the enemy did not have the Key and maybe, just maybe, one of them had managed to escape. It would have been nice to have known, in the end. He gripped the console, releasing another flourish of agony. Latt moved forwards. He was going to kill him.

This was it, this was – hello? What was this?

Something unexpected began to happen. The klaxons of turmoil lessened, and in their place came the *taste* of gold, the sensation of the first light of dawn. It was unexplainable, fantastic, *invigorating*. It flowed like spring sap through his veins.

The corners of Scara's mouth twitched for a split second. Had it worked? He dared to hope She was here. His grip increased on the console, the bones of his fingers knitting neatly back together. He could feel his wounds begin to close. He had a chance.

High above, golden light enveloped the watching girl, making her shine like a fallen star amid the swirling water. Fresh corals of a thousand colours erupted into life along the glass channel, building a spreading reef that gorged on the ethereal light that spilled from her.

Meris's mind was a battleground. Her own thoughts and memories blended with those of her ward. She saw grey skies filled with burning zeppelins, heard the roar of distant cannons, felt the touch of warm skin, remembered swords and fins and gills and claws.

She was lost amongst it all, a flame besieged by a galaxy of moths. As the world inside her mind tore itself apart she fought to hang on, to keep whatever connection existed between her and the man below. She could feel his pain recede from her, the shadows that fled as she approached. *She could do this*.

Meris wept silently, tears falling free from her to descend into the concrete abyss below.

"Kill him." Lott demanded of his brother, "Fuckin' kill him, Latt! Jus', jus' fuckin' do him!" His teeth ground with rage and his mouth frothed like a scrapyard dog, hindering the eloquence of his request.

"Pack that in, will you!" snapped Latt, brushing spittle from his collar. Once again, Lott fell obediently silent and cast the blackest of black looks towards the watching Scara.

Lott was tempted to get his rifle, and do him in himself - what was Latt waiting for? He'd wipe that smile off of the Captain's face, with a handkerchief made of hot lead! He clenched his fists. He might be sans-rifle but he still had his hands and made to use them. He had had enough. This bastard didn't know where the Key was. Maybe nobody did!

Their agent should have sorted this. If she knew where it was, then she should have got it herself.

Scara smirked at him.

"Right, that's it!" Lott cried as he barrelled forwards, fists raised.

"Fuckin' stay there, Lott!" Latt commanded, slamming his arm against Lott's chest in a way that declared in no uncertain terms that he was officially putting the kibosh on his brother's pugilistic plans. "Can't you see he's just trying to bait you?"

"Yeah," Scara croaked, blood settling in a fat gobbet on his lower lip, "stay there, that's a good boy."

"And you can fuckin' shut it!" Latt raged as Lott pushed against him, bellowing expletives.

Latt and Lott exchanged volleys of enraged snarls. Scara ignored their quarrel. The blood had slowed its exodus from the wound above his eye and now squatted, coagulating, upon his brow. The flesh had already begun to heal, the swelling receding. His skin itched as his wounds knitted together, the tissues shivering and melding beneath his torn uniform. He could feel Her now; the voice inside his mind spoke to him with greater clarity than ever before. She was here.

Something glowed faintly amongst the eaves, twinkling on the edge of vision. His gaze returned to the dust covered tiles at his feet lest he look up, and give Her position away.

He suppressed a hopeful smile. He had a chance.

A shoal of brightly-coloured fish skipped through the water, reveling amongst the spreading reef that spread out from where the girl shone amongst the current. Meris sieved through a kaleidoscope of mental images, hunting elusive scraps of meaning through the twisting maze. Crimson bursts of anthropomorphised pain called out to her as she flowed through his mind. She probed them gently, fusing bone and sewing skin with the same grace with which she grew the flowers in her hair. A small smile hovered upon her lips. *She could do this, she could help him.*

Concentration teased her brows into a frown, as she set to work.

–::–

Above the girl, unseen amidst a bower of hanging algae, a tiny sensor stirred into life. Clinging to the highest of the stone arches, cloaked in shadow, it took a reading.

[BEEP]

Several nanoseconds passed as it compiled its report and, after an infinitesimally tiny pause, it was sent. The data zipped through the aged communications network, plunging down through the Institute to rouse one of the dozing mainframes below. [BEEP], confirmed the mainframe, although slightly slower and with a bit of a wheeze. [BEEP] It yawned, and sent a number of commands to its colleagues throughout the building.

The sensor tapped a virtual foot, irritated by the unreasonable millisecond-long wait.

New orders flooded its miniscule console, and with a happy grin it flicked on a very small blue light.

–::–

A knife twisted in Scara's ankle as the bone creaked into position. He timidly added weight to it as the burning pain fled from him. His thoughts swam as She passed through his consciousness, soothing him like the rose-tinted memory of young love. She was here, She had sent him Her gift, and he would not fail Her.

He feigned a groan of pain, leaning heavily against the console.

"Ok boys, you got me," he coughed, pulling his face into a perfect picture of defeated despair. One of his hands flapped in a submissive sort of way, "you win, you got me, maybe I do know where the Key is."

The brothers' argument evaporated, grins settling on their grizzled faces. Latt sneered with sinister satisfaction. "You fuckin' coward," he spat, his face filled with disgust before breaking into a smug grin, "Y'see Lott, I told you deep down he wasn't the Billy-fuckin'-big-bollocks they said he was. At the end of the day he's just another dandy fuckin' coward." He clapped his brother upon the shoulders, his grin widening.

Lott licked his lips in a rather disgusting way. "Fuckin' Scara, Captain of the Ninth and Commander of the entire fuckin' Institute, what a wanker."

Scara weathered their laughter well. He straightened, making a big of show of it. "Ah, so you've heard of me, then?" he bowed slightly and slipped a sneaky arm behind him. He suppressed a smirk as his fingers twiddled at the fold of a diagonal pocket, concealed above the small of his back. A long-bladed knife, professional and veteran, awaited his bidding within. "Now who wants to guess where the Key is hidden huh? Any takers?"

Scara risked a newly-restored smile, "Lott?"

Meris span and swam in a world of celestial light. Her heart soared as she chased the last injuries away. She laughed and cheered within her mind, delighting in the energy that rushed through her. *She could do more.* The words sang in her head. *She could do a lot more.* Mending broken things, that was easy now; that was only the beginning. She could take these broken things and make them better. She could make them stronger than they had ever been before. Her heart drummed within her slender frame as she drew from the water around her. Unseen threads of vibrant energy cascaded from the river, pouring into the man below.

"Bullshit!" Lott bellowed, "Bullshit, he don't know nothin'!" Scara became the picture of innocence. His body buzzed like a kicked hornet's nest, eager for action. He was strong again, but not the strength he was used to, oh no. The energy and vitality of youth swelled his muscles, filling his heart with laughter. The aches and limitations that came with middle-age evaporated like dew before the dawn of a long-past summer's day.

"Look at him!" Lott cried, "He don't know nothin', he's stalling!"

Latt stepped forwards, his face contorting as his grim smile fought with a barely-subdued scowl.

"Lott, for fuck's sake, of course he knows where it is. This cold fucker has used it before." The scowl directed at his brother became a goading smile as his attention descended like a flock of vultures upon his captive. Scara's expression hadn't changed, however the unmistakeable ashen-grey of guilt tainted his features.

"Now come on Scara, what the fuck have I got to do?" The gun twitched before the Captain's face. Indeed, the fact that a gun of that size was still held in such a position added further testament to the bearded man's impressive upper-body strength. "What the fuck have I got to do to get that fuckin' Key?"

Lott fumed, his impatience threatening to shake him apart. "Jus' fuckin' kill him!" he cried, throwing exasperated arms upwards, "He's fuckin' about. Kill him and we'll grab some other boffin, he can't be the only one of them that knows where the Key is. Captain-fuckin'-

Scara or not, we've been at this for days." he fought to make himself sound reasonable, "Fuckin' kill him and we'll try someone else."

Meris was fully immersed, now; she looked through the Captain's eyes at the two bulky brothers that menaced him. For the first time, she felt complete; this was her purpose, it was clear to her now - to bring life, to restore life, to bring light to the world, to save them, to save them all from what they had created. She would redeem them.

And then maybe, if she succeeded, she would have her fuzzy, wuzzy bees. She smiled at the thought of that.

Scara's face twisted into a smile, a smile not entirely of his own creation. He had reason to smile; he was Captain Horatio Scara, decorated hero, leader of the Ninth and a veteran of more wars than he could remember. His fingers closed about the handle of his knife. He was outnumbered, outgunned, and was going to get out of this alive.

"I said SHUT UP!" Latt screamed at his brother, before turning back to Scara. Sweat beaded across his head. He had the gun, he had the captive, he was about to win the war, command the Purge and be the big hero. He had won; he held all the cards. "So why the *fuck* are you smiling?" He bellowed, waving the hand cannon wildly.

As one, Scara and Meris took a half step forward. He slipped the knife from its sheath, waiting for the opportune moment to strike. "That's right, Little Lott," Scara grinned dangerously, "shut that pretty mouth of yours, there's a good boy." Any second now...

"Fuck this!" Lott roared, his last nerve snapping audibly. He charged into his brother, tearing the gun from his grasp. Scara leapt, his body rejuvenated. He was quick; he was skilled. Lott staggered backwards, fumbling with the gun as Scara's long knife flashed towards him.

Man and girl cried together as they moved as one, bringing the blade around in a perfect and professional arc.

Lott's fingers closed about the trigger. He fired.

Scara never stood a chance.

Twin explosions left the barrel, firing a duet of heavy bullets. The first cleaved through Scara's mouth, splitting skin, rending muscle and spraying teeth. The second arrived a split second later and, buoyed by recoil, pushed into his forehead; erupting out of the back of the Captain's skull in a festival of bone and gore. Ghastly chrysanthemums splashed across the computer bank, eliciting sparks and acrid smoke from the proffered keyboards.

[INCORRECT INPUT – PLEASE ENTER KEY], it asked again.

DATA TRANSCRIBED FROM THE VIDI-LOG OF:
Captain Horatio Scara

**DATA RETRIEVED FROM [CLASSIFIED], STATUS:
NON-OPERATIONAL**

DATA RETRIEVAL DATE: [CLASSIFIED]

We have a new Master of Engineers, a woman by the name of McClusky.

She came highly recommended; though the modest nature of her prior work had kept her off of my radar.

Already, she has proven her worth. Her handpicked team took over executive running of the systems - a bloodless coup that ruffled a few feathers - and have been working to improve the internal communications network, as well as finally reactivating the Systems Monitoring Droids. With the help of the SyMons, overseen of course by an appointed administrator, progress on the MERIS project has increased by a significant percentage.

Finally, a damn 'bot that does what it is supposed to.

I never approved of the battle cogs Command insisted we took into battle. I would be foolish to deny their firepower, but what good is a soldier who seized up every time a bit of dirt got into the clockwork? Worse, when they were operational, the smoke from their exhausts ruined your lungs almost as much as they ruined any visibility.

Despite her best efforts, McClusky has been unable to get the automated defence network back online. She claims it is awaiting a command that she does not possess. I have given her a command of my own; she will not cease working on it until this Institute is a fortress once more.

I have yet to receive word from Command, and I am now greatly concerned. Gladstone is a master of efficiency; she would not allow so many messages to go unanswered. The broadcast network we had tapped into is now silent, nothing but static.

I have been assured by McClusky's team that this is likely down to a change in wind drawing radiation away from the Tsong rivers, disrupting the transmission.

My instincts are not appeased by this explanation.

We have a single aerial scout vehicle remaining operational, and I intend to make use of it.

I have given the order that First Lieutenant Chilvers is to take the ASV to Command HQ and re-establish contact. He departs in the morning.

We cannot allow ourselves to remain isolated.

Chapter Five

MERIS screamed as she was torn from the broken body. Her world collapsed around her, forcing her back into her own fragile form. She writhed in agony as the once-gentle light receded into her, striking her flesh like lightning.

The dead man sagged to his knees, his ruined head trailing like a lost dog behind him. The defeated torso sat there for an eternal second before slipping sideways, settling with a vacant weight amongst the grey dust.

Lott and Latt paid no attention to the corpse, for something else had drawn their attention. The murderous brutes looked skywards towards the vaulted ceiling, to the hanging glass river and the dimly-glowing girl who sobbed above them.

"Fuck me, it's Her." Latt broke the silence, his mouth opening and closing like a gasping trout, "They did it, they fuckin' did it!"

Lott's lips trembled as he stared at the forlorn creature in unusual silence, smoke trailing wickedly from the gun in his hand.

"What are you waiting for?" his brother cried, breaking him from his trance, "Shoot it!" Latt tore across the room to where his brother's rifle hung across the door handles.

"Uh, y-yeah, right!" Lott stammered.

He closed an eye, stuck out his tongue and flicked the

setting to automatic with a grubby thumb. He breathed out, took aim and squeezed the trigger, letting loose a full magazine of ravenous bullets.

Meris shrieked, marshalling herself as best she could, as gunfire erupted from below.

She dove beneath the water with the grace of a hunting kingfisher, barely raising a splash as she was embraced by the river. Beneath the surface her human form dissolved, a shoal of golden-and-black striped fish boiling from her fading body. As a single writhing mass, they twisted through the water, fleeing from the violence that coursed upwards.

Behind them the bullets found their target, stinging the reinforced glass channel like iron wasps. Through myriad black and beady eyes, Meris watched with horror as a firework of cracks sped across the glass surface, water already hissing down into the abyss of the hall.

The brutes whooped in unison as the glass river exploded downwards, its shimmering bounty hanging in the air for a terrible, frozen second before crashing onto the steps in a thundering torrent. A number of the aged supports twisted and split, tilting the remaining part of the channel onto its side, haemorrhaging gallons of water into the hall.

Latt laughed, his voice loud and joyous in victory. Brandishing the retrieved rifle, he fired several shots of his own at where Meris struggled in the rip-tide. At the foot of the stairs Lott leapt upon a convenient pile of rubble and danced an impromptu jig. "We got 'er brother, we got 'er!"

The discarded body of Captain Scara rolled into a supine position, buffeted by the crowd of small waves that spread across the floor. Scarlet blood coiled like smoke, mixing with the grey debris that had caked the floor to form a macabre soup around him.

"Come to daddy…" Latt leered hungrily at the dissolving girl as she fought against the tide, "c'mon now!"

There was much eager rubbing-of-palms.

Meris's hundred little hearts pumped in their chests, as she gulped water through her gills. The current roared all around her; a transparent riot of aquatic hands tugging at her fins, desperate to drag her down to where the wrong 'uns waited.

She focused her thoughts, morphing the shoal of glittering fish into three larger and sleeker silver bodies that battled the tide with spear-shaped heads and spiky whiskers. Together she pressed herself forward in a rotating diamond, using the slipstream caused by each of her bodies to help the one behind.

On the far side of the hall the severed half of the glass river hung limp like a brace of slaughtered rabbits. Its remaining brass supports twisted and groaned painfully as it vomited more of Meris's precious river across the stone tiles. A klaxon sounded, sending a trilling and definite note echoing through the hall.

A second siren answered it. Amongst the distant wall tiles, a salt stained brass hatch screeched as it broke free from its rusted restraints. A green box light illuminated the word [SEALED] above it as the door slammed into position, locking the remaining river behind a protective metal barrier. On the far side of the room, the last of the water fell away, sliding down the severed channel like a struggling conversation.

The now-isolated river groaned again as two more brass supports twisted and snapped, whipping through the air to lash wildly against the wall tiles. The ones that remained put up a valiant effort, but eventually succumbed to the unreasonable weight of their burden. The pair below scattered as the mid-section of the glass monstrosity tore free, shattering across the wide stairs in a maelstrom of spinning shrapnel.

Meris cried as loudly as her three sets of nonexistent vocal chords would allow. Her wide mouths opened and closed desperately. Any second now the second klaxon would sound, sealing her in the hall and leaving her to the mercy of those below. She concentrated; six lidless eyes trying to close as best they could. She strained for a new shape, yearning for freedom with the same vigour she had roused when trying to save the life of Captain Scara.

Poor Scara. Her futile attempts to save him had left her exhausted. Her mind fogged, the last of his memories clouding her vision. She saw fire and mud, faded photographs, rose petals and smoke. Poor Scara.

"No, Meris!" she commanded in trio, "Focus, focus!"

The rusted hatch, pitted by fledgling coral polyps and slick with clinging algae, waited just before her. *'Come on Meris'*, she urged herself, *'you can do this'*. Her three bodies shimmered and coiled around each other, twisting and pushing to become one; a serpentine, shark-like shape with a mottled pattern of deep green spots above a powerful, mustard yellow breast.

"I can do this!" she declared with selachimorphine determination.

The second siren sounded, announcing the closure of this segment.

'Come on!' she cried, silently, from between serrated rows of jagged teeth. Above the water the green light flickered on. Meris's lithe body cracked through the body of water like the tip of a whip. It was a desperate and last-ditch effort that took her from the vault, and out into the darkness beyond.

The door snapped shut with a hiss and a clunk,

isolating the hall from the rest of the Network and barely missing the quivering tip of her pointed tail. The Brothers Bad groaned in tandem as their prize escaped them.

"Fuck!" raged Lott. A lone bullet that had missed the earlier salvo was rudely ejected from the magazine and pinged off the closed hatch. "Fuck, fuck; we almost had her, fuck!" He rubbed his head angrily, and cursed some more.

"Enough of that, brother." Latt called out in response, descending the slippery steps with care. A knowing and unpleasant grin slithered about his bearded chops, "We'll still get that monster - oh yes, we'll get her."

Lott shrugged, and growled out a sigh - which is not as easy as it sounds.

Latt made straight for the fallen captain. "Alright Scara?" He leered, prodding the body with the steel toe of his boot. "You in over your head, eh?" The brute let out a satisfied laugh at his own lame joke, and was joined by his cohort in a dastardly duet of ugly chuckles. "Now, about this Key..."

Lott watched with a broad grin as his twin rummaged about the Captain's person. Latt's fingers plunged through the layers of waistcoats, over-shirts, under-shirts and a redundant armoured vest; scrabbling like hungry carrion birds at buttons and toggles. With a single motion the strong man unceremoniously tore the vestments away, revealing a bare and bloody chest.

"Well, well, well, who'd have thought it eh?" Latt leaned over the torso, addressing the suspicious lump that brooded just below the late Captain Scara's collar bone, "Clever bastard." He prodded at it roughly with his finger, "Chuck us that knife, will you Lott?'

Lott paused for a second, thumbing the hilt of Scara's knife that had mysteriously found itself attached to his belt. The ornate and well-esteemed weapon exchanged hands. Latt went to work, parading a wicked smile as the blade sank into the still-warm flesh. He jerked the knife sideways, cutting a rough arc around the rectangular bulge. The parcel was extracted carefully and held aloft. Blood dripped from its smooth sides, peppering the pale torso. Latt took up the knife once more, slitting and peeling back the layer of cream wax to reveal a delicate Bakelite box.

It opened with the whisper of a click, a work of art held within a crude grasp. The Key was extracted from its aegis with much elation and fist-pumping. It dangled from a silver chain, an ornate electronic memory device engraved with a delicate pattern of loops and swirls fashioned into the shape of a rain drop, a shed tear.

"Get in!" cheered Lott, hopping from his island of rubble. He landed amongst the murk runoff with a splash and put the boot in again; the rotter. "Cheers Scara!"

"Aye, cheers Scara." echoed a laughing Latt, the remark cast casually over his shoulder as he made for the muttering computer bank. The keypad became stained with blood and filth as various buttons were pushed. A reluctant hatch opened slowly, halfway up the nearest stack of consoles, [INCORRECT INPUT – PLEASE ENTER KEY], moaned the ever-flickering screen.

Latt paused for a moment, turning the Key in his fingertips like a diver who has found the perfect pearl. This was it, it was over.

His face set, his eyes growing dark as he slid the Key into its waiting slot. The computer whirred with surprise, clearly expecting its request to go unfulfilled. It pondered for a moment as it perused the data files. Well then.

The computer searched some distant servers, made a few calls and drew up a program. Numbers and letters swam across the screens as it worked, pixels mirroring the fish that once swam above it. Latt drummed his fingers on the console as Lott admired the ever-changing cyber shoal that danced before them.

There was a mechanical sound somewhere distant, a recording of something being unlocked. Another hatch opened on the console releasing a slender clockwork arm that proffered a very large, and very dangerous-looking red button. Above their heads a single, ominous word flared into life; [PURGE?]

"Oh yes," Latt rubbed his palms together and Lott licked his lips, neither action being particularly attractive. "Oh yes indeed!" he repeated, jabbing his thumb down onto the big red button, "Purge!"

DATA TRANSCRIBED FROM THE VIDI-LOG OF:
Captain Horatio Scara

DATA RETRIEVED FROM [CLASSIFIED], STATUS:
NON-OPERATIONAL

DATA RETRIEVAL DATE: [CLASSIFIED]

Chilvers departed without incident, though this was to be expected.

Progress is accelerating at a pleasing rate. I find myself growing more and more interested in the project as it develops.

The regeneration matrix was completed several weeks ago. Porvine explained the details as per usual, though the overview was not too hard to understand.

A demonstration was held in the main hall, in front of the great fountain.

Porvine, McClusky and I stood upon the dais as a young technician set up the equipment. The crowd numbered over a thousand, a mass of humanity that filled the surrounding halls, walkways and balconies. With the perimeter secure, I authorised the main doors to be unlocked to allow an extra hundred or so at the back, and welcomed the breeze they let in.

We stood behind a low table, an array of screens above our heads. McClusky was clearly uncomfortable in the spotlight, though unsurprisingly Porvine drank it up. His oration was filled with promises, and great sweeping statements of salvation. I was less convinced they would succeed, but nonetheless interested to see the demonstration.

A glass dome, filled with water and surrounded by sensors, had been placed upon the table. Inside, the brown skeleton of some deceased water plant hung limp. An opening, stoppered with an orange bung, sealed it within.

The crowd were shown slides documenting the project thus far, while an army of technicians prepared and operated all manner of monitoring and recording equipment.

I stood with my arms behind my back, my chest laden with polished medals, my gaze fixed over the heads of the watching crowd and through the towering doors, tracking the movement of thin clouds as they skulked across the yellow sky. My years as an officer have left me well equipped to deal with such pantomimes.

Porvine's speech ended as a technician, clad in heavy rubber robes, waddled over from the wings. In his black-gloved hands he held a pair of tongs, and between their pincers a pearl-hued bottle wobbled precariously.

I instinctively took a step backwards, a move McClucky mirrored. Porvine had no such concerns, and would have carried the thing himself had procedure allowed.

A second tech assistant removed the bung and moved away as the bottle's contents were poured inside. The crowd held a collective breath as the golden liquid flowed into the water. You could have heard a pin drop.

The reaction was incredible.

The liquid exploded into the dome, shining so brightly it was almost painful to watch. It swirled about like oil, before soaking into the rotting brown leaves. Immediately they burst into bloom, the dead vegetation peeling away to make room for the wriggling mass of fresh, green shoots.

The hall rang with cheers and applause. On stage, our faces split into grins; mine included.

For the first time it seemed that actual progress was being made, that they were getting closer to actually producing something of worth. I thought that perhaps their plans were not as insane as they appeared.

Now, I am not so sure.

The sound of cracking glass silenced the applause.

Within the dome, the plant continued to grow. Its leaves became fat and swollen, a menagerie of grotesque flowers pulsing along the stems like boils. There was another crack as a thrashing stem slammed against the glass.

The guards I had stationed around the stage turned their weapons upon the table, waiting for the order to fire. Their increased efficiency from the new training program is impressive.

We stepped back as the dome shattered, spilling water across the stage as the plant continued to expand,its bloating body consuming the table beneath it.

Porvine approached the flopping plant, cooing and wringing his hands like a concerned father. My warnings to stay back, to keep clear of the mutated specimen went unheeded. He called to his staff, demanding various monitoring and preservation equipment be rushed to the hall.

It was already too late.

To the dismay of all that had gathered, the plant died quickly. The speed of its growth was matched only by the rate of decomposition. Within seconds the green giant had wilted, its leaves and stems turning brown and black.

The sickly sweet stench of rot filled the hall as the crowd were instructed to disperse, and the experiment was closed.

Morale will be an issue in the coming weeks.

I attended the meeting that followed. Control and balance are key to the success of the project, so Porvine maintains. The matrix needed a host, a body, a mind, intelligence to judge when and how its target was repaired.

That is why they need MERIS.

I am still unable to ascertain if Meris is a name, or an acronym.

At this stage I am reluctant to admit my ignorance.

I will continue to observe.

Chapter Six

MERIS plunged into the glass labyrinth of rivers and pipes. Her gills clawed hungrily at the surrounding water as her heart threatened to burst from her chest. The shark-girl sobbed as she swam, which is not an easy thing to do underwater.

Burning rooms and war-torn floors flashed by, like cells in a film. Beyond the glass, the invading Reds continued to fight the desperate Blues in ignorance of the influential and frankly game-changing goings-on above. She travelled unnoticed by those without, just one of the millions of fish that thrived in the sprawling system.

Darkness gathered in gloomy councils as she descended into the depths of the Institute. The sounds of battle were smothered by increasing layers of concrete until at last, silence fell upon her. The reefs and shoals thinned, replaced by streamers of brown algae that hung like human hair from the glass. Grey shrimp and white crabs squatted amongst them, collecting the scraps that drifted down from above. They vanished as she passed, whisking away into hidden boltholes.

Pain and exertion choked her thoughts like thick smoke. Meris felt the bullets burn through her flesh, through *Scara's* flesh. She was fractured and lost, more than ever before. He was still there; faint on the edge of hearing, his final thoughts and echoed memories wandering through her mind like lost ships on a becalmed sea.

Meris shook her head, trying to dislodge him and feeling guilty for doing so. She had tried to save him; she had done all she could. Tears crept from the round discs of her eyes, dissipating into the water. She didn't know if sharks could cry, but that certainly wouldn't hold her back. The final earthly seconds of Captain Scara played themselves adamantly across her vision. She shook her head again, silently pleading with them to stop.

Lacking a neck, this motion caused her entire body to twist and thrash in the water.

It was in this fashion of frantic fin-flailing that the girl found herself paddling down an open channel of slow-moving water. Meris the Shark exhaled, and in doing so became Meris the silver-skinned girl once more. Her muscles cried out, protesting against the demands she put upon them. Her mind, overwhelmed, hung with despair as she drifted through the tepid stream. She allowed the current to push her, buffeting her numbly against glass walls thick with decaying algae.

This section of the Network hung beneath a curved gantry that encircled a truly enormous round room. The world beyond the water was a shadow-haunted vision of scientific ruination. A great tree, an eldritch construction of metal, rubber and glass burnt black by long dead flames dominated the room. Smaller machines huddled about it like worshippers before an altar, gouts of blue and white sparks erupting from their wounds.

A bank of monitors crowded above this particular section, hissing static at the water below. Like so much flotsam before her, Meris found herself discarded there by the sluggish current. A blanket of brown scum fluttered across the water, clinging to the forlorn girl that floated in its midst. She closed her eyes. Above her, the screens flickered and flashed desperate islands of light in the smothering darkness.

She wrapped her arms around her knees, drawing them to her chest while small, red finned fish seeped from her exposed flesh. They glowed faintly around her, scuffling through the drifts of detritus that swept across the glass floor.

"Meris." a distant voice pushed through the air, warped and distorted. Something flitted across the struggling screens. Monochrome pixels twisted, as a desperate image fought to retain its shape.

Meris's head lifted from upon her knees and tilted it with suspicion. "Hello?" she called into the darkness, threading harder tones of bravery into her exhausted voice, "Who's there, hello?" Beneath the surface the small fish huddled together, their eyes wide as they pulled greyish water through their panting gills.

The void swallowed her words. She bit her lip. Her shoulders rose from the water as she peered into the shifting shadows that prowled beyond the struggling limits of static glare. "Risss..." the voice, low and coarse, hissed around her. She turned as a face flared across the screens above. "Meris." the voice whispered from hidden speakers.

The girl suppressed the startled shriek that frothed inside of her. In the distance the tree roared into the night, breathing a plume of flame into the heavens. She dipped into the festering mire, slipping into the safety of its miasmic embrace, leaving only violet eyes shining above the scum.

On the screens, a ghost flickered amongst the static.

"This is an emergency broadcast from Captain Horatio Scara, Commander of the Institute Defence Force, transmitting on all available support frequencies." His voice echoed throughout the Institute. His face, free from the suffering that had been inflicted upon it during his captivity, looked down from the spreading vines of display monitors that clung to the concrete walls of the sprawling complex. The back-and-forth exchange of munitions between the opposing forces of Red and Blue ceased momentarily as all eyes turned towards the televised address.

"If this broadcast has activated, then the Institute has fallen and the Purge has begun. The MERIS project has failed. I repeat; the MERIS project has failed. To the survivors of this war, on whichever side you are on, I implore you to run. What we have created here is a threat to all life on Earth. The Purge cannot be stopped, it cannot be reasoned with."

Meris watched with fascination as the man onscreen spoke to the world. His features were marred by defeat, his words heavy with a solemn sadness. She rose from the water, sheets of scummy slime slipping from her shoulders as she moved towards the image on screen. The water frothed around her as aquatic hands bore her aloft. She mouthed his name, her pale hand raised towards his image.

His head bowed beneath the weight of his words, "We have failed. It is my hope that the measures we have taken will be enough to contain it within these walls, though nothing within will survive. You, all of you, must leave this place; find a way off of this island. The Purge has begun - you must take flight, you must flee, you *must*, you, y-."

Meris rushed across the slow-moving water, and towards the nearest screen as the message began to decay.

"But how?" she asked aloud, her voice echoing through the darkness. At her feet ripples clustered where she trod upon the liquid surface. "Scara..." she whispered his name as if breaking taboo, "How can I..? How can I escape?" The ruined labyrinth of brick and glass was all the girl had ever known, a prison of both the body and mind. The outside world was an almost impossible concept, an alien realm, nothing more than changing pixels on grime-covered screens.

The image on-screen began to warp, the words blending together into a barely legible post mortem monologue, "MERIS ta -flee a-, flee, find a way ta-, find-the. Li- lie, lie. Riss, Mer."

"What?" she cried, shaking the monitor, "What are you telling me?" Grey and violet eyes met, locking across the abyss. Meris' mind raced as she tried to decipher the dead man's message. She tried to probe the data sequence, moving out of her own self to preserve the message.

"Find a, find a way- flight, light, li-Risssss." Before her the face began to fade, the words reducing even further, the voice drowning beneath an eventide of static. She thought desperately of a way to hold on, to stop him slipping away again.

"MERIS," Scara's final words hovered on the edge of hearing, "MERIS, a way, find the, the light."

The image vanished, and the screens fell silent.

"No!" Meris cried aloud, her porcelain skin ghostly white in the gloom, "Please, I don't understand, I-"

A deep klaxon sounded in the distance. Dust trickled from the concrete heavens as elephantine soundwaves stampeded throughout the sprawling complex. Two spherical lights, shackled to the grey bricks within rust-encrusted cages, answered the bellowing call and erupted into life. Their red glare drove against the shadows, breaking them against the distant walls and twisting the mechanical tree into a grotesque abomination lit by hellfire.

Meris tore her eyes away from the dead screens, as from behind the tree's upper branches, the Portrait was drawn out from the darkness. The serene figure walked as if amongst flames, the crawling light highlighting her unnatural splendour with a thousand bloody shades. Her almond eyes blazed defiant, the white and violet bright against the ebb and flow of ruby light and pitch darkness as the lamps pulsed below.

The girl clenched her fists, replaying Scara's final words in her mind. "Find the light." she whispered, before allowing the stream to swallow her.

—::—

Latt turned his back on the brobdingnagian bank of buzzing screens that had so recently broadcast Scara's address to the gathered horde of red-hooded hoodlums. "He's a smooth-talking fucker, ain't he lads? Well, he used to be." He barked a laugh from his spot on the makeshift stage and jerked a thumb at the frozen face behind him. The crowd cheered and waved a menagerie of banners and rifles with gusto. They'd been cheering a lot lately, their elation bolstered partly by the demise of Captain Scara but mostly by the free flow of complimentary celebration hooch that had been liberated from one of the Institute's storerooms.

"Flee?" He mocked, "We get all this done, and he wants us to flee? What do you think boys and girls; shall we do what the good Captain asked?"

A shuddering blast of boos shook the hall.

"Or shall we do what we came here to do, and kill their monster?"

The cheers and applause were almost deafening. The crowd were frenzied, their bodies humming with bloodlust and booze. Steam rushed from the rattling pipes above their heads, obscuring the soot-blackened ceiling with fragile wispy clouds.

Latt strode the faded wooden stage, his arms wide and wild. "That's what I thought! Flee? Fuck that! For too long have we fought this war, fought and bled to stop these loons, these madmen!" Spit frothed on his lips as he gestured to where blue-coated bodies hung between two bubbling boilers. "No more lads, no more! There's only *one* left, *one more* life to take. Are you ready?"

The crowd cheered their assent. There was more weapon-waving and the odd gunshot. His brother Lott straddled a rickety fold-up chair, nodding and grinning with every word.

"I said, are you ready?" He egged them on, his thick arms gesturing at them. The theatrics were apt, and perfect for what he was about to do. He drank in the thunder of their applause, his smile growing so wide as to split his face.

"And who are we going to kill?" he whooped, wiggling his eyebrows and kicking his legs as he gambolled across stage.

"The MERIS!" No word had ever been shouted louder. The crowd erupted into dancing, and whooping and waving their red flags with limitless enthusiasm. Their leader harnessed their raw emotion and flung it back at them, causing them to wind higher and higher into euphoria.

"The MERIS," Latt jeered, "their monster, their abomination, our so called saviour! Well, fuck that! Let's get this show on the road, eh?" The noise of the crowd shook the fixtures and fittings as he approached the console, his name being chanted by a thousand mouths.

This machine was a distant relation of the earlier computer, an ugly contraption of levers and buttons surrounding a grubby convex screen. Two green words flashed upon it, a question;

[COMMENCE PURGE?]

His hands coiled around two levers. He licked his lips, "Let the Purge begin!"

A great bellowing boom erupted as the two levers were slammed into place. Black smoke belched from rattling exhausts, rising above a blinking bank of glaring crimson lights. The great machine rattled and writhed as sluices slid open and riveted tanks, festooned with all manner of warning signs, began to gurgle and groan.

All eyes raised upward, to pumps and generators sweating a rank miasma from their sagging iron bellies, adding their foul vapours to the fustiness of humanity that clogged the domesticated hangar.

A great twisting web of pipes trembled as a toxic brew of chemical nightmares pumped through them. They converged with an audible sloshing at a central point, before rushing down towards a lumpy spigot.

Their collective breath was held, and immediately regretted considering the poor quality of the air in there, as the first droplet of ominous blackness quivered on the lip of the spout.

It shivered, it stretched, and it dropped.

Spindly arms struck out from the shadowy mass as it convulsed through the air, scrabbling like an upturned beetle.

The loudest cheer yet roared to life as it exploded into the water. Behind the glass the foul thing slithered, turning a horrid little cartwheel as shadowy tendrils emerged from it. The first droplet was followed by a second, and then a third. A foul carnival was had as the rest of the Purge was pumped into the unsuspecting river system.

Latt watched with hungry eyes as a free droplet propelled itself over to a worried-looking patch of yellow algae. If an amorphous blob of concentrated evil could grin, then this little amorphous blob of murk would be a regular Cheshire Cat.

It struck the huddle of xanthophytes like a cobra.

His beard rustled around a wicked grin as the algae withered from the strike, dissolving into a drift of grey ash that trickled from the glass.

"We've got 'er now." he chuckled to himself, "Oh yes, we've got 'er."

DATA TRANSCRIBED FROM THE VIDI-LOG OF:
Captain Horatio Scara

DATA RETRIEVED FROM [CLASSIFIED], STATUS: NON-OPERATIONAL

DATA RETRIEVAL DATE: [CLASSIFIED]

Here I commit my account of the Incident within the Main Birthing Chambers on date: [REDACTED]

Porvine's personal valet came to my quarters in a state of excitement, begging that I attend the latest activation personally. I initially refused, following the number of failed activations that had occurred since the last debacle.

Porvine assured me this activation would be different.

I had already seen the reports. Annotated sketches, like something out of Da Vinci's sketchbook, have cluttered my desk. The files are full of images of men and women, of body parts and machines melded together.

I was never a fan of science fiction.

I begrudgingly accepted this latest offer, if only to put an end to Porvine's endless messages.

The activation was supposed to be classified, though despite my best efforts it was hard to impose much in the way of data security in such a close-knit warren. Without the outside world as a distraction, everything was worthy of gossip.

Therefore, I was unsurprised to find the pathways to the birthing chambers a hub of activity. It seemed as though every hand had descended into the vaulted halls beneath the Citadel, causing the decorated walkways to groan under their weight.

I was pleased to see my men were already engaged in crowd

control. They had cleared a path to where Porvine, McClusky and their retinue waited. I nodded my approval as I passed.

The flabby scientist swelled with pride before the arched entrance. On my command, a detachment peeled off from holding back the crowd and flanked us as we passed between the reinforced plate doors and entered the secure chamber beyond.

Porvine raced ahead, his robes flapping wildly behind him as the doors were closed and the electrolocks sealed us in. He chattered incessantly, McClusky and I strolling in his wake. Technicians flocked around him as he reeled off the specifications behind what they were about to achieve.

It was all Greek to me, though I do not doubt McClusky understood more than I. Still, I was under no illusions as to what I was about to witness.

They were trying to birth a god.

A great, treelike contraption of wires and steel filled the centre of the hangar-sized room. Even here the glass canals hung from the vaulted ceiling and threaded between the twisting metal branches.

The walkway that we climbed encircled it, giving the scientists access to its many levels. Thick bolts of electricity slithered down from a distant transmitter in the ceiling, their snapping coils illuminating the room with a fierce light that stained the air with the taste of tin.

Across its trunk, amid a nest of monitors and twitching robotic arms, hung eight cylindrical pods. Within each one, floating in a glowing blue liquid a pale body lay still, as though sleeping.

Even from a distance I could see that they were unnatural, somehow utterly wrong and completely perfect at the same time.

It was hard to describe.

The sight of them raised the hairs across the back of my neck. I could tell my men felt the same way; I took some reassurance in that.

The technicians did not seem to share in our discomfort. They worked as though they were no more remarkable than a doorknob. It must be something you grow accustomed to with time.

I did not, nor do I now, intend to grow accustomed to them.

—::—

It was Porvine that suggested I took a prominent role in the activation. It would look good to have the Commander of the Security Corps throw one of the main switches, he reasoned; it would show I had faith in the project.

I protested and tried to relinquish the role to McClusky, who held more responsibility for the machine's construction than I. She declined politely, agreeing that it would be good for morale.

I have been reduced to keeping up appearances.

—::—

We were shown to the control booth, a small reinforced room riveted onto the side of the curved wall and accessed by a raised walkway that rang beneath our boots.

A large viewing window dominated the wall of the oval room. Through it, we were afforded a complete overview of the facility. The tree's branches rose before us, dwarfing us to reach up towards the reactor. A million lights winked across their metal surfaces, relaying data to where the pods hung from the lower boughs.

The rest of the lab hummed like a hornet's nest as technicians made final preparations. The atmosphere in the control room, however, was strangely muted. Clerks sat in silence at green-lit monitors, confirming results as they flickered up the screens.

Only Porvine mirrored the energy below. He flew about the room, disrupting the work with endless questions he already knew the answers to. Lightning flashed across his glasses, turning them into bright blue discs that hid his watery eyes from me.

More than ever, he reminded me of one of those mad doctors from the pictures. McClusky and I tried to keep out of the way as best as possible.

An hour passed before I found myself at the controls. My hand rested upon the thick lever that would begin the activation. I recall how my skin itched at its touch, my palm sweating onto the ridged rubber handle.

Porvine stood beside me, gripping the second lever with childlike glee. They were designed to be pulled simultaneously.

A green light flared, signalling we were good to go. I nodded to him, lending silent dignity to the proceedings. Porvine clearly lacked any sense of decorum or tact. He was consumed by pomp, crying something bloody stupid as the levers descended and the great metal tree burst into life.

The generator above us roared, flooding the room with a blinding white light. We were shielded by the tinted viewing window; those outside had been provided with darkened glasses ahead of time. Fat coils of electricity swarmed across the branches, the crackling serpents moving with fresh purpose into pointed nodes that studded the spreading contraption.

The sound of whirring machinery filled the air as an array of bound glass baubles filled with golden fluid were drawn from within the bowels of the machine, and twisted into waiting recesses around the chambers. Their contents sloshed wildly before draining into a thousand needles, sat poised and ready to deliver the solution into the sleeping bodies.

A collective breath was held as the vast machine followed

about its surgical routine, each movement deft and calculated for exact precision.

The first scream, when it came, was deafening.

It struck us like a physical blow. Along the gantries, the crowd recoiled as the first of the creatures erupted from sleep.

It thrashed uncontrollably within its pod. Muscles bunched across a torso so flawless it could have stood on display in a gallery. There was a grinding of machinery as it tore away the steel implements that pierced its artificial veins. Its gaze turned to us, its eyes burning with violet fire. Its scream became a snarl, hands forming glimmering fists that beat upon the walls of its glass prison.

My men reacted quickly, raising their rifles and taking aim, awaiting the order to fire. We looked on with gritted teeth and streaming eyes as more of the sleepers awoke, their warped screams fusing into one as they fought to escape their shuddering cells.

The alarm had been triggered, the klaxons sounding from the rafters. Those among the civilian staff who had not already begun to flee did so, the sound of feet racing across the raised walkways beating like kettle drums.

A small security detail pushed through the crowd and surrounded Porvine, McClusky and me, insisting I flee with the civilians.

Unarmed, I had no choice but to reluctantly join them.

Porvine protested as I gave the order to fire. His voice was lost beneath the sound of gunfire. The first volley found its mark, the bullets spilling golden blood from a shimmering torso as it pulled itself through the glass.

It fell with an unearthly shriek, its form shifting and twisting into a thousand shapes before breaking across one of the thick roots that held the tree in place. It reformed in seconds, a writhing mass of limbs twisting like a golden squid amongst the tangle of sparking machinery.

Two more had already escaped their holdings and leapt like apes onto the gantry. They shifted form, snatching up stragglers in talons and claws as we escaped through the pressure hatches.

Gunfire rippled across them, tearing through the smoke that billowed from the damaged chambers and drowning my orders to retreat.

The dying cries of my men, as the deadlock seals span into place, will haunt me for the rest of my days.

What have we done?

Chapter Seven

MERIS twisted in the water; Scara's final words, his message, sat on her lips.

'Find the Light?' What did that even mean?

She hovered at a cross section between two connecting pipes, the ruby lit laboratory left far behind. Thick glass ballooned out around her, the outside murky and distorted. Banded brass riveted the sections together converging on a rusted honeycomb of mismatched tubes that twisted away to a hundred different destinations.

Long fronds of greenish brown sargassum weaved a basket around her as she sat crossed legged, a pensive look upon her face. 'Find the light', she pondered, 'hmmm'.

A shoal of small, silver fish; slender with orange and blue fins, dropped out of a barnacle clustered outlet. They flitted about, catching the wan light that streaked through the milky glass.

'Excuse me,' she waved at the newcomers, 'do you know where the light is?'

Though it was immediately clear that they didn't, they were more than happy to dance wide loops around her as she puzzled on the choice ahead. The fish joined her as she drifted towards the nearest tunnel.

She sniffed, 'hmmm'. The water coiled; uniform and uninteresting which was probably a good thing.

What does light smell like?

Her thought caught in the minds of her followers. As one they trickled forwards, flashes of sliver flowing across her arms as they moved towards the cluster of gnarled pipes. She could almost see through their eyes, their twittering thoughts echoed in the back of her mind.

Meris watched as they twitched through the opposing streams, fighting the suction from one while riding the flow from another. 'Come on', her whispered words of encouragement quivered through the water, spurring their senses as they moved this way and that, 'find the light'.

Her piscine companions conferred, their writhing bodies forming a collective ball that bobbed and dipped as they argued back and forth. Meris hovered nearby, optimism bright in her eyes.

There was a movement behind her.

A wide mouthed fish with fins like paddles dropped out of a dented funnel. It flapped wildly, its saucer like eyes swivelling as it careened through the water. Meris ducked as its gold and brown body passed overhead. The smaller fish scattered, the shimmering ball exploding, their connected minds evaporating as they fled into the warren. Meris recoiled, swimming clear as the intruding ichthys clanged against the riveted brass. It thrashed briefly before diving into the darkened mouth of one of the lower tunnels.

As she watched its tail disappear into the gloom two turquoise cuttlefish sped past, trailing bubbles like the tails of cephalopodic comets. She twirled in their wake as they raced around the dome before taking separate routes into the rest of the Network.

A shoal of red fish followed them, splitting as they disappeared into the hive. Meris turned, the pitter-patter of tiny fins growing from the curling channels behind her as more frightened fish poured into the curvilinear cross section.

She threw up her arms as the stampede struck.

A blizzard of scales filled the water as the kaleidoscope of aquatic life whirled around her. Metallic bodies bumped and buffeted her as the super shoal fought to pass into the waiting tubes. The scent of fear poisoned the water, the taste oily on her tongue. Meris curled into a ball, gritting her teeth amidst the storm, as the press of fleeing fish broke around her.

They cried to each other as they swam, a single word repeated by a thousand silent voices; 'Flee'. A red light bloomed in the distance, its beams sneering across the curved glass. A second followed it, burning directly above the brass bound junction, spilling blood red light through the transparent walls.

She lifted her head, shielding it with an arm as she peered through the mass of bodies. This light, this burning glare that inspired such fear, could not be what she sought.

Around her the fish increased their barrage, pushing together in tighter formation as they struggled to escape into the glass labyrinth below. Lidless eyes shone bright with hell fire. She closed her own eyes before them while panicked piscine screams flooded her ears. 'Flee,' they begged her, echoing Scara's message, 'flee'.

Her heart beat heavy in her chest, rising dangerously towards her throat. 'No' she breathed, the word torn away from her by the scaled stampede.

Deep within the living tomb the first warm glimmer of golden light blossomed across the girl's skin.

Meris clenched her fists as she steeled herself against the endless maelstrom of aqua fauna. Her mind began to spread, saffron once again tinting her vision, while invisible motes of consciousness burrowed unseen and unhindered through the layers of flesh that encased her. She leaned into the shoal, steeling herself as she pushed against the scale clad maelstrom.

Golden light shrouded her now, her form lost in its embrace. The rays reflected from a million tiny scales as she sent her will leaping through the water, focusing it into an almost physical presence to hold back the vile red glare. Her muscles burned, twitching as torrents of energy raced through her veins.

Meris opened her eyes and exploded.

The shoal recoiled from the blast, thrashing away like shards of stained glass. The hole left by the detonating damsel wavered briefly before collapsing under the unrelenting press of pushing bodies.

Meris, freed of human form, raced forwards as a glowing spectre that leapt from fish to fish like living lightening. They convulsed as she passed through them, a cold blooded shudder that flowed through the struggling shoal.

Hard plated eyes, dark voids set amid fluorescent flesh, rolled and swivelled. Through the twitching discs Meris watched the submarine world flicker by like snippets of a half formed tale, echoes of a forgotten harmony. Gates of brass flashed passed as she sped down the wide tunnel from which the shoal funnelled like rainbow tinted blood in an artery of glass.

The ghostly girl coiled through the tube, surfing through the marine menagerie with ease.

The fish glowed around her, bright with energy as she moved with their muscles. She felt their fins flare at her touch; wide and strong, slender and sleek, pulling desperately through the water to escape. Escape from what?

Meris frantically probed the minds of her hosts as she passed through them.

'Flee', the shoal's collective subconscious continued to cry. 'Why?' she called, spinning as she slipped from the body of a slender, hook snouted fish. She twirled through the water, formless before splashing into the side of another; long finned and round scaled. She called again, her question repeated. 'We flee', came the answer, desperate and dulled, 'we all flee'.

She passed from body to body, a flashing mob of shapes and sizes.

Her question repeated again and again, though their answer remained ever the same.

Shoal mentality. One fish sensed something, saw something, and dashed for safety. Its movements, erratic and unexpected amid the placid reefs, startled others that followed suit. Panic could move through the water with the potency of any predator, alerting the senses and feeding the fires of hysteria that could turn entire shoals into desperate writhing masses.

The tempest that thrashed about her was more than this. This panic was sustained, it was real. Their fear was driven deep within them like an iron nail, firm and unwavering, forcing them forwards. The bulging tube boiled as whole levels of the Institute were drained of life, the inhabitants of the Network joining together in a desperate exodus into the depths.

Anger simmered inside of her, sending crackles of electricity bristling through her. She half reformed, her fists balling, her eyes filling with fire. 'Why do you flee?' she demanded, erupting into a human shape that burned amid the shoal. 'Tell me, why?'

'Purge', the answer came, from every voice at once, striking the shoal like a hammer blow.

The Purge; a word so ominous it was capitalised in the mind of any who thought it.

They chanted the word as Meris smouldered beneath the water, her form rippling as piscine bodies swerved around her. Sunset shades painted the tube in broad strokes of reds and gold, speckled by the shadowed forms of the fleeing fish. Their voices hummed; a pulsing, panting mantra that filled the brass bound cylinder. 'Purge', myriad voices cried, 'Flee, Purge, flee!' The words echoed through a thousand mouths, bleeding into the shared mind to dominate the world around her.

Louder and louder the word boomed. Meris closed her hands about her ears as the fish wailed and cried, 'Purge, flee, Purge!' She hardened herself against the panic, calming her mind as their screams engulfed her.

On and on it went, a drum beat, an endless flood of cold blooded bodies until at last, after an eternity, rippling cracks opened like dull blemishes amid the Technicolor tapestry and the shoal began to thin.

The crowd splintered into bustling blooms of colour that broke away like billowing ribbons of smoke left in the wake of a living locomotive.

'Purge', she shouted, scattering one such cluster, 'What is Purge?' Eyes that would have widened with fear had said eyes been of the widening sort glared back at her. 'Flee!' the usual response crawled through the water, 'Flee, Purge'. The word squatted before her as their fins disappeared through the murk of churned water. A galaxy of discarded scales surrounded her, winking like drowned stars amid the growing morass of sediment that glowed pink in the caged light.

Meris huffed and stared after them, hovering equidistant between the sloping glass walls. Here and there straggling clouds of brightly coloured fish whirled through the water, darting through the fog of sediment.

The pounding susurration of their cries dwindled as they flowed away and into the darkness. The girl called out to them, willing them to stop. Their feral panic hissed at her, beating back her attempts to slip into their minds.

She cried a ballad of frustration as they veered away from her, stamping her foot which is another difficult thing to do underwater. 'What is the Purge?' she asked of the now vacant tunnel, 'What are you all fleeing from?'

'Flee!' A voice, deeper and slower than the others, vibrated down the glass tube. Meris turned asa white shape appeared in the distance. A great fish, larger than any she had seen before, panted through the red tinted gloom. It approached slowly, swimming just a few centimetres above the glass floor. Grey sediment shrouded it, kicked up by its round and ridged fins. 'Flee' it growled, 'Purge'.

The fish cocked a thick plated eye, the speckled disc swivelling as it approached. Heavy black markings spiralled across its bright white flanks like storm clouds against a winter sky. Its massive v-shaped mouth opened and closed rhythmically; revealing rows of yellowing hooked teeth.

A chain of thin silver fish darted from one of the many cylindrical tributaries that opened onto the main artery, spiralling around her before vanishing into the gloom. Their minds cried as they swam, panic blurring their words into so much more white noise.

Meris' body flickered as the large fish drew close. It could be dangerous, it certainly looked dangerous. This could be what the others were swimming from, though somehowit didn't seem likely. Despite its monstrous size the fish sang of flightas earnestly as its predecessors.

She drifted forwards; she had to find out what this Purge was, where it was coming from, how to escape it? Maybe this fish, this fish of all fish, would be able to answer her? The panic that had clouded the minds of the shoal was conspicuous in its absence within the new comer. Instead it emanated anger, bitterness and pain.

It looked at her with predatory focus, her reflection shifting in the blackness of its eyes.

Meris pinned a friendly smile across her lips.

'Hi, fish!' she waved.

DATA TRANSCRIBED FROM THE VIDI-LOG OF:
Captain Horatio Scara

DATA RETRIEVED FROM [CLASSIFIED], STATUS:
NON-OPERATIONAL

DATA RETRIEVAL DATE: [CLASSIFIED]

We lost eighteen guards, and eleven members of the science corps.

Our meetings during the six days that have passed since the incident have been brief; he knows I hold him partially responsible for the deaths of my men.

The remaining responsibility is my own.

On my orders, McClusky has had the birthing chambers isolated and flooded. I have learned this will not destroy the creatures, but it will at least contain them until further action can be taken.

I have slept little; their violet eyes haunt my dreams, their voices call to me. I have ordered that entire section of the Institute to be quarantined until we have decided upon a resolution.

Porvine assures me that they have long held a contingency. In the case of emergency, the system can be purged section by section. I have authorised its immediate deployment.

Chilvers has failed to return.

Our scouts have also reported a vessel at the edge of our territory. We have been unable to identify it as friend or foe. I have increased the patrols.

The extra work will keep the men's minds from dwelling upon the events of these past days.

Chapter Eight

THE great fish growled at her. A riptide swirled around them as it puffed out its plated gills and swept its vast tail from side to side.

'Flee,' it boomed, its voice thudding into her chest, 'flee the Purge!'

'No please,' Meris approached cautiously, her hand outstretched in a generally calming way, 'I must know what it is you flee from? What is the Purge, why does it inspire such fear in the heart of the shoal?'

She swallowed, burying her fear, and placed her hand gently upon its snout. Dish sized nostrils flared as her slender fingers brushed lightly against the wall of scarred and pitted scales. This was a very old fish indeed. It bristled at her touch, sucking in great currents of water that caused her hair to whirl about her head.

The pale piscine pilgrim paused, giving the girl a desperate and fatigued look. 'Flee' it croaked the word, a definite instruction rather than just more mindless marine mantra. The word dripped wearily from its gargantuan maw sending a spreading sound wave to break against the curved glass walls. Its gaze rose from her and, with a sweep from its broad fanning tail, the giant pushed past her to continue its journey through the labyrinth.

Meris kicked after it, catching the ponderous behemoth easily. 'Wait' she called adamantly, 'please, wait!' She circled the curve of its gills to trot alongside it.

Wide eyed and wilful, cautious and curious; Meris ran

the back of her hand across the beast's huge armoured side. 'Please', she whispered softly, soothing the heartbeat of adrenaline that pulsed through her colossal companion, 'please wait'.

'Wait', it replied, its voice like two boulders grinding together at the bottom of a trench.

The fish's vast fins trod the water, undulating in the current like standards upon a battlefield. Meris smiled and adopted what she hoped was a sincere and trustworthy pose. The scales flexed beneath her touch, humming with a fierce energy, a defiant and proud.

She had felt this before; a steady and strong will, comfortable yet reliable, like slipping on an old, blue coat. She had felt this when she was, when she had been, when she had seen through his eyes.

No. And there it was; honeyed tones, warm silk memories, a hundred minds dripping the sweet nectar of distraction. This was the trap, her undoing by her own actions, to follow the glistening webs into the minds of others. Her own being becoming grey and still and useless while she lived a thousand other lives, watched a million other memories. No. She was in control. She would always be in control.

She closed her eyes, folding her consciousness within herself. She was not a man in a blue coat, or a bloom of coral or a majestic fish. She was Meris, her own Meris. Her skin glowed softly, lighting lamps across the fish's side.

The fish sensed the change in her mood. A torn dorsal fin rose in dull alarm, the thin white membrane strung between rows of semi translucent spines that arched across its back like spears above a shield wall. Meris turned her thoughts to it. Soothing sounds flowed from her lips, easing slightly the suspicious tension that gripped the giant. She took a deep breath as she drew her knees to her chest. It watched as she moved in front of it, hanging serenely in the water mere inches from its war scarred snout.

It was now or it was never. Meris whispered her name as an introduction, dipping her head in reverence of the brobdingnagian being. It felt like the right thing to do.

The fish turned its head this way and that, regarding her with those wide saucer eyes. All around them small puffs of fish darted in an out of the gloom, their cries hushed in its majestic presence.

'Gollollopp' the fish announced, the sonorous sound bouncing down the tube. It smiled, well insofar as a fish could, at the sound; pride shining amongst the contrasting colours that swept across it.

Meris attempted a clumsy curtsy. She could not slip into the mind of a creature of such stature easily.

The other fish, the small shoal dwellers or crawling crustaceans, accepted her as one would the embrace of a child; inevitable and harmless. For the most part they were simple creatures and shouldered the burden without complaint. Simple and good, she added with guilty haste, and did not begrudge her presence. She should not assume this to be the case with Gollollopp however. Such an imposition, if uninvited, could prove to be a fatal folly indeed.

'Gollollopp' she spoke its name reverently.

Gollollopp's grin broadened, its lips pulling back to display ever increasing rows of dagger like teeth. The girl set her own jaw firmly, staring into the two predatory voids that lurked deep within the dark pools of its eyes. Her hair coiled about her in the current as the seconds crept by like sea slugs.

'Meris', Gollollopp growled and after an uncomfortable silence dipped its long sloping head as best a creature with no discernable neck can.

The effect was instantaneous. Gollollopp's consciousness rushed into her, buoying her mind upwards as their thoughts intertwined.

'I am The Great Gollollopp', the fish boomed. Its words flowed freely through her, a mix of tectonic growls and jovial thoughts, 'Sire of Hundreds, Grandsire of Thousands, Warden of the Infinite Shoal and Lord of the Eastern Trenches!' Its ragged fins spread out from its face like slatted wings, swelling its already gargantuan form in an impressive display of biological engineering. 'And what kind of thing are you, eh?'

Meris lined a response up in her head, well aware that her private thoughts must be guarded lest she inadvertently cause offense to the regal creature. It too was suppressing dangerous thoughts, dark slivers of emotion that rippled beneath the surface of its words. She was careful not to chase after them; such an intrusion would surely end up with her becoming dinner.

'Hmm', Gollollopp hummed before she could offer an answer.

He swept forward, a dangerous smile creeping across his massive maw as he began to circle her. 'Hmm, hmm not quite a fish, not quite', Meris's eyes fell to the creatures teeth, each one as long as her hand. She raised her chin defiantly, hiding any weakness as he swept past her again.

If stone could purr the fish would have mimicked it perfectly, 'not almost a crustacean, a mollusc perhaps? Some new kind of sea slug maybe, yes? Surely not one of those ghastly dry things eh, one of those monkeys with two skins? Hmm, though I can see the similarities.' He winked a suspicious eye, an action that threatened to turn the lidless disc inside out as he circled ever closer. The water churned as his circuit tightened around her, brewing a mean looking vortex that played tricks with the crimson light.

A movement of his fins twisted his armour clad bulk, dazzling her as light gleamed from his mailed flanks. He always leans to the same side, the observation skittered through her mind.

'Speak little Meris', he snarled, 'speak and tell me, what are you?'

Meris suppressed a shiver of fear as his shadow passed over her again. 'Meris', she announced, her voice loud and clear, 'I am Meris.'

The Great Gollollopp laughed, a rough, geological sound, 'I know that, little Meris, that I know'. He darted forwards, displacing a wave of water, and gestured to his head with a fanning fin, 'I know who you are, you showed me who you are, but as to what you are? Hmm now, I don't know that.' He cocked his head sideways as he spoke.

Meris opened her mouth to answer. 'I...I am', she began weakly, the words fumbling from her lips. She was Meris, wasn't she? How did she know that? When did she know? Images rose like grey bubbles of from the depths of her mind, clouding the violet of her eyes. Steel machines crawling like spider crabs across pale, bloodless skin. She shivered, then and now, as their needle tipped fangs bored into the still flesh.

Eldritch chemicals seeped through coils of rubber tubing while flickering grey monitors showed visceral scenes of pulsing organs. She could feel them beyond the glass, masked and distant. Cold ghosts in white and blue, moving within a fluorescent tomb. She felt their early memories, the first minds watching from within her sarcophagus of plated glass. Their hopes and ambitions, petty jealousies and solemn secrets flashed, had flashed, before her eyes. In her prison she shifted and screamed, formless and unfinished.

She remembered the dreams, the ones she spoke to as

they slept. She remembered the gunfire, the searing pain and the desperate pleas, the fear of death and tiny acts of bravery.

The screaming lights and burning machinery; the blood in the water.

The Great Gollollopp watched through her eyes, his own swivelling in opposing directions. A sympathetic frown shuffled across his bulbous features. He ceased his circling, gliding through the water to settle into a lopsided bob. His thorn ridged lips quivered, his plated gills fluttering shallowly. Behind those bulging eyes a maelstrom of alien sounds and clouded visions tore at his piscine consciousness, their screaming talons racking oozing wounds of pure sensation across his mind.

A worried rumble sounded in his throat, shaking the curved glass, 'You are, you are alone'.

Meris flexed her fingers, the digits moving a mile away. A distant light shone in her eyes, a glimmering dawn that beat back the clouds that had settled upon her. Her cells twitched, they itched. Words droned around her, human voices raised in alarm, the chattering of a living reef, the songs of the shoals.

The water was dark; the kind of brilliant blue that the light dares not to touch. She felt the spines rise along her back, the ridges flexing as the current flowed across her scales. She yawned, an impressive motion that distended her tooth studded lips away from her wide and sloping head. Water rushed through her powerful gills, spinning in a slipstream behind her. She darted forwards as diffused oxygen exploded across the fluttering filaments that flanked her throat.

The first voice filtered through the expanse of liquid sapphire, a long note that rose and fell; the shouts of the Shoal's out runners, calling to each other across the open water. Her mouth peeled back, curling into a grin that crawled towards the edges of her gills. Other voices joined them, building a harmony that rolled back and forth until the water vibrated with their raised voices.

Meris called back to them, the sound thrumming from deep within her corpulent stomach to add bass notes to their jubilant song. Countless shades of blue danced around her, teasing and warping the melodies into new and fantastic combinations.

Contentment draped her flanks like a cloak, a warm pride that languished within her powerful muscles. Her fins spread wide as she dove deeper into the azure abyss. She called to them again, cheerful boasts and marine jokes; her deep voice filled with laughter. The Shoal replied in kind, their jovial banter pulsing through the depths. She could picture them now, clouds of deep silver bodies rolling over each other as they navigated the ebbs and swells of the Eastern Trenches. They called their names as they gambolled through the deep, a joyous chorus that flowed as they did; morphing into a thousand glittering patterns.

'Gollollopp' she whooped as the water rushed through her gills, 'The Great Gollollopp!' The Shoal roared its applause, the great pool frothing with their adoration as the sound rose like breaking waves. And then, something else.

The proud grin that split her face faltered. Something prickled along her lateral line, shivering across her spines. A new sound crept beneath the symphony, a disjointed tangle of disquieting notes. She swivelled her bulging eyes suspiciously, her ears straining to catch more of the curious chords.

There was a movement below her, a faint twitch, a coil of deeper darkness that twisted obscenely in her shadow. Her spiky grin twisted into a snarl. Something was encroaching on her territory, something uninvited, something foreign and fell.

Her nose pointed downwards as she dived down to meet it, her powerful tale driving her towards an unseen enemy. She called her name as she approached, confident her fearsome reputation would set any trespasser fleeing.

The shadow moved, an unearthly flickering shiver. She grinned. A pressure wave of water swelled ahead of her as she barrelled into the depths. The inky intruder recoiled at her approach, becoming one with the darkness that permeated the deepest recesses of the Trenches. Her eyes boggled, snatching at the light as she scythed through the blackening brine. Her fins paddled rhythmically as she twisted this way and that.

Meris's nostrils flared suspiciously. Beyond the sharp, familiar tones of brine something sinister lurked. The oily tang of decay peppered the water, the hollow stench of long death.

There! A brushstroke of pitch darkness streaked against the heavy blue gloom. She rushed it, her plated jaw set. Another snickered past. She swerved, snapping at its fading trail. A third condensed from the shadows, followed by a fourth. Meris growled as a flock of pulsating bloblets clustered around her. She flared her gills, fanning out her fins in what was an intimidating sight indeed.

They watched her sightlessly, whispering and jeering, undaunted by her display of marine might. She sucked in a great flow of water, inflating her stomach until it became a speckled beacon of silver and white in the darkness. 'I am The Great Gollollopp' she bellowed. The gloopish goons guttered as her voice boomed through them. 'Sire of hundreds,' she continued, scowling against the air of menace that bled from her oozing opponents, 'Grandsire of thousands, Warden of the-'.

'Hyundreddsssss' the word erupted around her, drowning her voice, 'Thyousenddssss'. Two billowing blobs slammed together, fusing into a fresh nightmare of scrabbling tentacles. She twisted in place, fins pedalling wildly as more of the amorphous monstrosities drew themselves from the darkness and collided into new and increasingly horrifying combinations. The water bubbled and boiled as the corrupt parliament of individual creatures collapsed into a growing abomination that brooded before her.

Serpentine syllables crashed into her ears. She roared a reply, challenging the writhing mass, the flapping of her mighty fins stirring a maelstrom about them.

The shifting wall absorbed her voice, echoing it back in twisted mockery.

As the last rogue globule was pulled into the rotting conglomerate, a split formed in its centre. It flashed across the surface, darting before an opening void that bounded through the quivering darkness like a pack of dogs. Meris backpedalled slightly; her sword-tipped dorsal fin rising in alarm as a menagerie of mismatched teeth pushed out of the fault line. Black saliva hung in ropes across the vicious lines of yellow stained fangs, stretching as it twisted into a malformed smile.

Meris snarled, baring her own teeth.

Beneath her shining armour of heavy scales, her muscles bunched as she took up a defensive position. Her great, sloping head thrashed from side to side as her tail beat upon the water.

'I am the Great Gollollopp' she shouted again, a challenge now, 'Lord of the Eastern Trenches. What vile manner of thing are you? What vile manner of thing trespasses in the waters of the Infinite Shoal?'

The creature's smirk broadened. 'Infinites', it sneered, the sound prickling through the deep, 'Yes'. A rotten looking tongue, grey and pink and knotted with pulsing purple veins, slithered out of its newly formed throat. The repugnant appendage tasted the water, flickering before her face before withdrawing into the grimacing maw.

'Answer me creature', she charged it again, a feint that stopped just before its shifting flanks. She snapped at it as she passed, her jaw closing millimetres from the mockery of flesh.

Meris gagged as the stench of the thing filled her nostrils. She fought against the fear that flowed through her veins, urging her to escape the abomination's presence.

It spoke as she rounded, preparing to charge it again, 'Yes, you are one, but they are many'.

Bloodshot eyes blistered its surface, reptilian; mammalian, piscine. Hungry pupils turned away from The Great Gollollopp and searched upwards to where the shoal swam on in ignorance of the terror below.

Their song had reached a cheery crescendo that danced through the water. Their words became whirling drumbeats, blaring trumpets, celebrations of their strength and freedom and longevity within their hallowed Trenches.

The beast turned, revealing a hunched back hanging with fatty pustules and writhing tentacles. 'Manyy', it cooed, its fat tongue dragging hungrily across what loosely could have been called lips, 'Let us leave this one small fish as witness, let this small fish see what death we shall bring, what doom shall befall the shoal of thousands.'

Meris' wide eyes widened further as realisation struck her heart. 'No', she roared, rushing forwards, 'creature stop, turn and face me'.

The twisted thing ignored her and continued its

journey into the light. Its body mutated as it rose, its form ever changing into increasingly horrid designs to aide its ascension. Ragged fins slid out of its bulk and thrashed upwards, lifting it through the churning water with surprising speed.

Meris charged after it, fighting to close that gap that widened between them. 'Coward', she snarled at its back, 'stop and fight me, coward, fight me!'

The Purge slowed, its warty tentacles flaring.

Red eyes popped across its back, a second mouth opening below them.

The great white fish burst ever upwards, spinning through the streams of toxic bubbles that followed in its foe's wake. The second mouth spoke, 'You are one and they are many. Though I search for the one, first many must die.' Its grin almost tore away from its vague attempt at a face. It began to laugh, a swollen choking sound, 'Yes, yes! I can taste their deaths, they will become beautiful, they will be Purged!'

It turned and rocketed upwards, its second face hanging down beneath it, the grin mocking her as it approached her shoal.

Meris body burned as she exploded through the water. Her teeth were bared in piscine fury, hungry to tear and rend the foul thing asunder. She closed in, swimming in its ever shifting shadow. The beating of her heart filled her ears while the taste of blood tinged upon her tongue. Her pumping fins threatened to split, the membranes straining between rows of spear tipped pterygiophores. The pained cries of her muscles went unheeded, blind to their protests her tail slammed back and forth throwing her after her prey.

'Face me coward' she snarled as her gills flushed gallon after gallon of diffused oxygen into her blood. A swarm of pupils locked onto her, the eyes pushing against each other as they clustered to watch her approach. Writhing tentacles framed them, spreading out from its expanding body.

'Face you?' the thing growled thoughtfully, 'Yes, small fish I shall face you. Come to me, come to me and embrace defeat.'

It laughed at her, the sound filling the water as she thundered towards it. Bubbles streamed from her, her voice a cry of war. This thing will learn of defeat, she swore an oath to herself.

Meris growled, her mind clouding as her thoughts were consumed by war. Let this creature of foetid night that dares threaten her shoal be broken before it. She would rend it from the world leaving nothing but dying rags. Her mouth opened, her teeth razor sharp and ready to tear it asunder.

Fire filled her eyes as she bore down upon her enemy.

The Purge smirked, extending a thicket of spindly legs from the base of its bulk, each tipped by wicked looking blades as black as night. Meris threw her fins forwards, twisting in the water as the lethal limb struck out like a scorpion's tail.

It was faster than she had imagined.

The creature gibbered at her as the striking spike pierced her side, tearing a vicious streak along her left lateral line. An agonised scream died in her throat, her voice mercilessly choked from her while iron hammers of pain beat within her chest.

Its laughter intensified as the Purge pulled its skewered victim towards its slavering maw. Fresh mandibles clicked together greedily. 'You are one', it sneered, 'one small fish, the one small fish that will watch as the many die. Listen to their screams small fish and know that theirs are only the first. Many shall die; so many shall die before I find the one. Though, for now, you shall not be among them.'

The purge chuckled as it retracted the loathsome lance. She grunted as it moved from between her ribs, expelling a thin string of blood that coiled about her lips. A thousand red eyes admired her pain, ceaselessly shifting across the writhing mass.

'Go now small fish, broken fish, and slink away. Let them die without their Great Gollollopp beside them, their Great Gollollopp whose weakness condemned them to death. Go now and let that knowledge guide you to your demise.'

Two great wings sprouted from it, larger than ever before. Meris' immobilised body rolled in its wake as it pushed itself towards the shoal above. Across its stomach a hundred eyes swivelled with delight as it soared above her, its mad words dripping giddily with grim satisfaction. 'Go on small fish,' it sang, 'unless you intend to watch? Shall you watch as they die, as all shall die?'

It shrugged, its body convulsing into a more streamlined shape. The foul mass of eyes and teeth that served it as a head turned to the light. 'So be it. Watch me now, small fish, watch how I kill them, watch and do nothing.'

The white fish gasped again, one fin pulling desperately at the water. Above her the Purge unfurled its vast fins and began paddling towards the surface, rising with lazy glee towards where the Infinite Shoal danced and sang in blissful ignorance. Her vision clouded, one side of her body becoming numb. Her tail batted weakly back and forth as she struggled after the ascending abomination.

Around her the songs of the shoal filled the water. She called to them, her desperate warnings falling helplessly into the darkness like autumn leaves. Blood hummed in her ears and tainted the water she crawled through. At her side, one tattered fin dragged uselessly above where thin strands of raw flesh pushed like fingers between her plated scales.

The fell creature was now a distant smudge, a dark stain against the aphotic greens and blues of the water above. Her body curved as she fought to stay on course. Frozen shards of pain sank into her muscles, spearing them in place as she tried desperately to keep moving. Her breathing was deep and laboured as the gill on her right side struggled to compensate for the damage to the left.

Her lips were heavy, her throat weak. She choked out another desperate warning, despair consuming her as it faltered, unheard. She struggled through a turquoise world. Sheets of pale light flowed down from above, fluttering into the deeps like ribbons of silk.

Meris moved in fits and starts, panting between each enervated burst of upward movement. The creature's diseased stench fouled the water, an acidic varnish that clung to the very molecules like biting ticks. She coughed as it crept through her gills, the trailing tendrils of rot caressing her tongue and seeping into her weary flesh.

The stars winked above her. Tiny pin pricks of light that tumbled down from the verdurous heavens.

They passed her by like snowflakes, white disks that turned over and over on their axis as they drifted into the endless abyss below. Meris watched as a porcelain sliver danced towards her. It span in place for a heartbeat, quivering against the deep blue before continuing its journey down into the deep.

Meris cried aloud, calling out to the Shoal as despair raked its frozen talons across her beating heart. They answered her at last; their dying screams filling her ears as the scales of her loved ones danced ever downwards into the waiting darkness.

DATA TRANSCRIBED FROM THE VIDI-LOG OF:
Captain Horatio Scara

**DATA RETRIEVED FROM [CLASSIFIED], STATUS:
NON-OPERATIONAL**

DATA RETRIEVAL DATE: [CLASSIFIED]

I command a circle of hell; what we do here is an abomination; what we do here will save the human race.

We returned to the birthing chambers to find them transformed. Through the plate glass viewing windows we observed a world born anew. The mechanised levels of the vault were now ablaze with all manner of marine life. Fish in their thousands swarmed in great shoals. The once-bare walls and tile floors were now lost beneath swaying forests of kelp and coral.

What remained of the fallen had been converted into new life. Its beauty made me sick.

The creatures have integrated themselves perfectly into the ecosystem. They are able to emulate their surroundings completely, slipping from form to form as easily as I put on a coat.

As such, it has become impossible to distinguish them from the natural fauna and flora.

Porvine has protested at length. Despite the loss of life his creation has caused, he pleaded that his experiment was still a success, that his creatures were controllable. His naivety has become intolerable.

I would not allow any more lives to be risked in pursuit of this fantasy. The Purge was initiated at 13:00.

—::—

What they have created is, to the layman, a 'living poison'. I had been assured that it was with good reason that its handlers nicknamed it 'the chemical devil'.

When I first learned of its existence, my mind turned to its use in the theatre of combat. I now know what a grave error it would be to unleash it upon the Earth.

The Purge was activated remotely, the codes held securely on a command key and readable only by the Citadel's main command computer.

Much to Porvine's distress, I had entrusted its activation to my lieutenant.

The old man wept as the black fluid was administered by a mechanised technician. The Purge reacted quickly, shifting into all manner of grotesque shapes as it cut a swathe through the flooded chamber.

It was lethal, utterly ruthless.

Whatever it touched was reduced instantly to bone and ash, and with each creature consumed it grew and became more monstrous. Within a minute it had swollen from a single drop, to the size of a horse; within two, its jaws could engulf an entire shoal of fish as they fled in vain.

The golden creatures, flushed from their sanctuaries, fought helplessly. They shifted from one form to another; giant crabs and malformed sharks, squid with hooked tentacles and great beaked turtles, stabbing and slashing at the growing mass.

The Purge, when it struck, was efficient; brutal.

Their screams pierced the glass, filling our ears and lodging deep within our minds.

We watched, gripped by horror, as their bodies were broken and consumed. Through the porthole one of them saw me, its violet eyes boring into me. It streamed through the churning water, flitting from shape to shape as it tried desperately to escape.

We heard its cries for help; we felt its inhuman words speak to our very souls.

The doors were deadlock sealed; there was nothing we could do.

The golden creature slammed against the door, begging as its fists beat upon the reinforced steel.

I stepped forwards, commanding Porvine to be held back as the creature's face appeared at the window. Its eyes, those two violet orbs set within a perfect golden face, topped by a seemingly endless flow of turquoise hair, pleaded with me through the glass.

She looked exactly like they said she would.

The Purge caught her quickly, a net of barbed tendrils burning into her flesh. Her dying scream marked us, damned us.

The Purge gorged itself upon the creature's limp body, many eyes turning on us as it ate. It watched us as though we were nothing but meat, cattle for the slaughter.

I held its gaze, I saw myself reflected in those terrible red eyes. Though it was nothing but a man-made device, I instinctively knew that I could not reveal the slightest weakness to it.

I dismissed the men, instructing them to remove all non-essential personnel until I alone remained.

I watched as it completed its grim task, I watched it grin victorious. I watched as, on my orders, it consumed our gods.

In our pursuit of divinity, we had synthesised evil.

Truly we are lost.

Chapter Nine

MERIS gasped as she was torn from the Great Gollollopp's memories. The noble fish watched as she rematerialized before him, her body forming from within a swirling shoal of lemon-coloured jellyfish. Squishy yellow bodies piled atop one another, bustling within a growing knot until the girl hovered in the water once more.

Tears like splashes of mercury dotted her lashes.

Meris banished them from her eyes as the giant's grief slipped from her heart. Now was not the time for her to weep. She rushed to him, any sense of fear stripped away. Gripping his mountainous face as best she could, Meris closed her eyes and pushed her head against his snout.

His proud head dipped thoughtfully as she traced the roughness of his battle-scarred scales beneath her fingertips. "Hmm," he broke the silence carefully, "Yes, you are definitely not a fish."

She pulled away. "I am sorry, Gollollopp." It was all that could be said.

The white fish regarded her, a human-shaped anomaly; lost and alone, an artificial life in an artificial kingdom.

"And I am sorry too, little Meris." He turned, revealing as he did so a puckered mass of exposed flesh, the jagged grey scar that marred his left side.

Her hands touched her lips as he moved away, her eyes wide; remembering the searing pain as the Purge tore through his body. His gaze fell heavy upon her. "Our bodies heal quickly; the wounds inflicted upon our flesh leave little but faded scars. It is in our hearts, and in our minds, where the true pain of our losses swims with us into eternity."

He spoke as much to himself as he did to the watching girl. In the glass tunnel, hung with the grime of the fleeing fish, he seemed smaller. His high-finned back was turned to her now, the vast paddle of his tail sweeping steadily back and forth. His mind pulled away from hers, the mental threads that tethered them thinning like a spider's silk.

"Please, Gollollopp let me help you." She raised a hand in his wake, golden light already blossoming between her fingertips.

It reflected in the great black discs of his eyes as he cast a look back at her. "No." he rumbled, "I wear the mark of my failure with me, little Meris. I will not dishonour them by hiding it."

Meris lowered her hand, the light snuffing out like a candle. "I understand." she nodded, the words almost true.

She swam beside him, forcing her eyes not to dwell on the fish's ruined flank. "How do we honour those we have lost?" The question went unanswered. The Great Gollollopp's cragged nostrils flared, his gills grinding the water around them.

'What is it?' she whispered. Meris resisted the temptation to reach out a reassuring hand, to look through his eyes. She had still not earned that right. The gargantuan fish bristled, his muscles taut beneath his monochromatic armour. His telescopic eyes fixed deep into the silt-clouded distance.

Meris mirrored his gaze, but could see nothing. "Gollollopp, please." she asked again, tendrils of fear coiling in her chest, "Tell me what you see, what is it that troubles you?"

"Flee." He commanded, his voice a stone wall. "It is coming - you must flee."

Meris' heart raced in her chest. "What is coming?" she whispered, knowing the answer. The fish remained focussed ahead. "Gollollopp, please..." she swallowed, trying to keep her voice steady. "Tell me, Gollollopp!" Her voice rising, "You must tell me what is coming!"

The answer tainted the very water itself.

Around her the world began to descend into darkness, the shadows twisting into nightmarish things as though the mere thought of its nature could summon it. Her flesh crawled beneath her skin, twisting and writhing as if it fought to escape from her. She turned as a chittering, chattering susurration bled through the water. It crawled and pulsed like a living thing, the squabbling of myriad horrors.

The Great Gollollopp moved forwards slowly, his fanning fins pulling him carefully through the water. "Go now." He ordered, "You do not stay." His words rasped against her mind firmly as the last connections between them were severed. Meris retreated slightly, heading towards the exit the shoal had passed through into the network of twisting tubes.

"No," the fish growled, casting a look backwards, "do not follow shoal." His fin flared out from his side, ragged flesh clinging to the exposed spokes. Meris' eyes followed the gesture to a mollusc-clustered faucet, lurking between fluttering fronds of dark green weed. "Go there, go now."

"Gollollopp!" Meris called to him, her voice swirling

down the glass tube, "Come with me, please!"

Fresh leaves coiled around her ankles. Her essence filtered into them, surging down their stems and causing them to flare out behind her; a deeper, thicker forest of green flourished behind her pale, flowing tunic and that undulating mass of turquoise hair. Hope shone from her eyes, and played upon her lips as she implored him to flee with her. "Please!"

"No," He growled, looking over at her for the last time. "I stay. I fight. I die."

Die. The word hissed through the water.

The encroaching sound rose, filling her ears. *Die, die, die!* A thousand unnatural voices called the word, corrupting it and spitting it back in mockery.

"Yesss..." The caustic chorus coagulated into a single menacing voice. Red light erupted from a nearby lamp, loosing a burst of crimson flame as the shadow oozed into the far end of the brass-bound pipe, a tail of noxious fumes billowing in its wake. A lumpy head, all teeth and jowls, pushed itself from the mass. Nostrils opened up alongside a rising crest, sucking wetly as it sniffed blindly at the water around it. "Yesss..." It hissed, as a wide mouth ripped across its blistered black flesh, "Yesss, die!"

A corpulent stomach sagged from beneath its newly-grown spine, quivering with excitement as the solidifying smoke pushed it forwards. A claw-tipped arm reached out, scratching for purchase as its iron hard nails scraped down the curved glass. A second ghastly hand grabbed onto the brass banding, its muscles bulging as it squeezed its unctuous body through the riveted ring and into the tunnel proper.

The Great Gollollopp puffed out his gills and flapped his fins in an impressive display of princely piscine power. "Monster!" He bellowed, moving to block the line of sight between the abomination and its target. "Face me, filth. Come to me, monster, come and fight!"

He snapped his jaws, the sound clapping like thunder over the sinister chorus that emanated from the creature.

The Purge vomited throaty laughter; its vile maw spreading, sprouting broken teeth like mushrooms along a rotting log. The ridged nostrils opened and shut as it sniffed towards the direction of the sound.

"Ah, yesss..." Fleshy red eyes burst across its malformed face, rolling in warty slackened sockets to smile greedily at the snarling fish. "Small fish. I remember you, small fish... I remember your fear, I remember your pain." An oily, bloated tongue, covered in pink suckers, slithered from between the ranked rows of mismatched teeth and out into the water, wriggling obscenely as it tasted the air. The tips twitched happily, before retracting back into the fatty folds of its throat. "I remember them as well, small fish. I remember the sound of their screams; I remember the taste of their flesh. I remember as they called out to you for salvation. They screamed as I took their words from them, they wept as I took their minds."

It laughed again, prowling ever closer on its menagerie of limbs.

The Great Gollollopp roared, lashing out at the waters with his fins. Meris felt the hatred and rage that consumed him as a warm buzzing at the edge of her senses. The fish leapt, its muscles releasing and throwing it towards the vile creature that taunted him. His lips pulled back, white teeth flashing in the gloom.

The Purge dodged easily, its body dissolving into a billowing cloud of grey smoke. Its laughter echoed louder as it took a lazy swipe with a half formed claw, missing by inches as the Great Gollollopp twisted out of its reach. He turned and dove forwards, passing through the Purge's dissipating trail as it danced around him.

Meris watched in horror as the creature solidified before him; its malleable flesh stretched into the form of a massive eel with scales as dark as the deepest trenches. A wall of twitching flesh formed between her and Gollollopp, filling the tube with its foul body. The malignant creation struck again, lashing out with its spiny tail. She cried audibly, stepping out from amongst the forest of curling fronds as the valiant fish was slammed against the thick glass walls.

The Purge cocked its head at the sound. Its long snout swung around to face her. Banks of nostrils opened and closed, its tapering jaw opening into a serrated smile. Its tongue flickered out again as nine eyes moved across its face, clustering together to form three burning red orbs that glared at her with an insatiable hunger.

"What's this, small fish?" It asked, its tone jovial as it snatched up the Great Gollollopp. The injured fish groaned as the Purge coiled its tail around him, the spines piercing his armour to burrow into the flesh beneath. "Another of your shoal?" It cooed, a crown of horns sliding out from behind its head, "The last of them, one I missed at our last meeting, hmm?"

The creature slithered forwards, its plated stomach rippling through the sediment that spilled across the glass floor. It sniffed again, a thick and snorting sound. Meris watched, transfixed as those eyes bored into her, the pupils cutting through the shifting reds like blades of purest night. "Oh ho, small fish, what *is* this?" Its tongue flickered with excitement as it sought out her scent. "What have you got here? This now, this is something *new*."

The jagged grin widened, its eyes bulging as realisation settled upon it.

The Purge snapped back to the struggling Gollollopp.

"Now, now, small fish. What have you got here, hmm? What have you brought me?" It tightened its grip, extracting another pained cry from its captive. The writhing body twisted as its eyes locked back onto the watching girl. It inhaled deeply, before the thick rumbling continued. "Oh yes," it purred, "Small fish, small fish, you have done so well! *You*, of all these small fish, *you've* found my One. I took your many, and in return you brought me one, the One!" The rubbery tongue played about its reptilian lips, slithering between glistening stalactites of dagger-like teeth, "I can't tell you how *pleased* that makes me."

It flowed and dribbled down the tube; the Great Gollollopp, still ensnared in its coils, trailed behind it.

Meris set her jaw as it approached. Her hands became fists at her sides. "Purge." She addressed it boldly, her voice firm as she desperately suppressed her nerves. She tilted her head, radiating defiance as she glared into its eyes, "Release him."

It ignored her. Sinewy arms slid from its sides, gripping the glass walls as it drew its face closer, a slender, warty neck slithering from freshly-sprouted shoulders. The tongue flourished before her face, thick knots of veins standing out against the rotten pink flesh. Its face bobbed before her, dancing in rhythmic serpentine motions.

"What was that?" it smirked, cocking its head.

A pulse of golden light bloomed in her chest. Meris' violet eyes narrowed. "I said, release him!"

"Exquisite!" The monster chuckled softly, maintaining its hold on the struggling fish. Mandibles slid from its jaw, clicking eagerly. "Such bravery for something so small, so fragile. You *do* know that I can taste your fear, don't you? I can smell it! Oh, little thing, you hold so much fear within you. It is glorious!"

103

It pushed forwards, swimming past her before looping back around. The vile being quivered as it spoke, the barbed spines flexing grotesquely with each word, "Meris. That's what they called you wasn't it, little sister, hmm? The MERIS?"

Three eyelids slithered shut as it savoured the word.

"They poured so much hope into you, little sister, and so much fear. I see, yes, I see now why they sent for me - why they unleashed me to cleanse this world of water and metal and stone. They fear you, little sister. They fear your *power*." The word echoed against the glass walls. "Can you not feel it? Can you feel it burning inside of you, gnawing on your bones, clawing at your flesh?"

Its voice crept across her skin; probing at her mind with tiny sucker-like mouths. She drew a cover of leaves around her as disembodied eyes giggled in the water. They orbited her like burning red moons, oily black skin folding over lenses alive with malice and greed.

"So much power, trapped inside something oh-so-small. Do you think they planned for that, little sister? Do you think they knew?" She closed her eyes to its words that swarmed like grey fog around her. The Purge's form wavered, tendrils of darkness curling from it to probe at the shining creature before it.

"Release him." She demanded through gritted teeth. She felt herself harden, down to the cellular level. A fire billowed within her, funnelling through her veins to prance across her skin. It kicked and spat at the circling darkness, snarling defensively at the probing shadows.

Meris furrowed her brow, fighting to keep her form intact whilst the crackling maelstrom danced around her. Her body shook in position as bones shifted within the flesh, fighting to be free of this human shape and away from the loathsome beast that attempted to infiltrate her psyche.

In a smatter of moments Meris mastered herself, her body burning bright with golden flame as the water around her began to boil. In the green gloom of the tube, tinted by the red bulbs and tainted by the Purge's musk, she shone like a beacon holding back the night. The vile creature stared into the fire, its tongue flicking along its edges. The fish snared in its coils continued to struggle, unseen, as the wretched wyrm danced before the simmering ball of light.

"Come now, sister." The words pierced the roaring flames that crashed against the weathered rocks of her mind, "Do you really think your little light show can keep you from me? I assure you, it shall not. I was made for you, little sister. I exist to bring an end to you. Allow me to demonstrate..." The Purge reached forwards, a razor-tipped claw passing effortlessly through the fire. Black flesh bubbled and spat, blistering, melting and reforming as it extended the hand to her face. Tails of soot-stained smoke spilled from its hooked talons as they closed around her chin.

The pain was unimaginable.

Meris fought against it, a biting cold that gnawed at her thoughts and spread like shards of glass through her muscles. Old wounds opened within her, the agony of bullets tearing through Scara's flesh returning as fresh and raw as ever. Gouts of flame erupted across her body, burning brilliant white where the Purge's claws pierced her skin.

Her pale flesh recoiled from it. Veins of golden light rippled beneath her skin as she pushed against its foul influence. She tasted blood in her mouth; her own. A copper piquancy tipped with an aluminium zest. Her ears, too, beat with the stuff, their rhythmic drumming punctuating the Purge's ever-present hiss.

Her vision turned inward as she was engulfed by fire. Within her mind grey spots stained the saffron clouds, corrupted motes of the Purge's vile ordure that worked to infect and consume her thoughts. She threw up more barriers against it, casting back the darkening clouds with the last of her strength.

At the edge of her mind, the Purge seemed to extend forever; an endless mass of darkness choking the life and light that once surrounded her. The beating essence of the Network was shut away, sealed behind a toxic curtain. Now there was nothing but emptiness, a vacuous void containing only endless hunger and multiform malice.

She struck out as it closed around her, throwing back the smothering veil with surges of honey-coloured lightning that twitched and span through the blackness. Motes of consciousness rode along them, fractions of her mind that coursed a hazardous trail through the stifling night. The effort paralyzed her, her physical body freezing in place as the Purge closed about her.

The battle for her soul raged within her mind. The sound of thunder rumbled in her ears as the dark clouds swept about her.

Another bolt leapt from her greying skin, spinning through the crashing tempest. She sent another flurry of thoughts out into the world, each an inconsequential particle of her consciousness that carried a single question on its pilgrimage. "Where are you?"

Meris whispered this to herself, the words shrouded and buried, sequestered away from the Purge's pervading presence that roared around her body, "Gollollopp, where are you?"

The Purge cooed softly, paying little heed to her attempts to hold it back.

It murmured in obscene mockery as it tasted her

memories, savouring her many lives as it squirmed deeper into her mind. Its burning glare filled her vision now, wreathed in thick smog that settled on her thoughts. "You... you who has seen so much, lived so much, experienced so much. Little sister, what have they made in you - what have they made for me?" Its distressing eyes bulged, the words dripping drunkenly from its malformed maw, splattering and spreading across her shivering skin.

Her body sagged as the Purge's crushing weight took its toll. The abomination's motes of corruption had now grown into a vicious suckling siphon that plunged into the depths of her, drawing out the myriad memories of every creature she had swam with, every flower she had blossomed and the human she had died alongside. She felt the numbness nibble at her fingertips, creeping around her extremities like scavengers circling a fresh kill.

"Yessss..." It slathered, drinking in the feeling of fresh, uncurling petals. Its tongue thrashing grossly as it gnawed at the memory of her swimming with a small band of large-eyed catfish, enjoying the carefree joy she felt as they rooted amongst the sediment in search of their next meal. "More," it croaked, maddened with gluttony. "Give me *more!*"

Meris' breathing grew shallow as she forced more of herself out and away, riding tendrils of lightning in futile attempts to escape her assailant. Water flora blossomed beneath her, climbing from where the crackling lines of living fire struck the glass. They grew quickly, vibrant islands of rippling greens and warm browns that fluttered defiantly before succumbing to the ambient pestilence that strangled the waterway.

The Purge swayed in its nightmare kingdom of shadowed water and ruby-hued glass. Reptilian arms clad in spiny crustacean armour peeled away from its bloated sides. It drummed its foul fingers across the swelling plates of its stomach as the intoxicating effects of the struggling prey filled its malodorous form. Greasy eyelids closed in ecstasy as it greedily devoured the sensation of fresh water sliding across a basking turtle's back.

Fat flippers slapped against the glass floor, rising clouds of sediment that settled grey and brown across its festering flanks. "What a meal they have made for me, little sister, what a prize you are!" Its body uncoiled as it gloated, rubbing against the glass with abhorrent glee.

Forgotten, the body of the white fish fell into the dust and lay still, strangled and discarded.

–::–

Meris's bones twisted inside of her, begging her to change form. Those parts of her body that remained free of the Purge's blighted grip churned in agony. She suppressed a scream as the monster tore through the layers of her mind, pushing deeper into her soul. A spark of it left her lips; a tiny, yellow jellyfish-like mote of thought riding a twinge of electricity that skipped beyond the reach of the Purge's devastation.

A slow trickle of bloodstained water pushed through The Great Gollollopp's plated gills. He shuddered. A weak ripple passed through his fins, lifting his tail for a struggling second before collapsing back into the dirt. His eyes clouded, sealing him within a lonely cell of broken bones and pain. The world around him faded into little more than a blanket of darkened shapes, lit by a faint golden light that flickered in the distance.

"Meris..." he croaked the name. The noble fish tried in vain to rise for the fifth or fiftieth time since he was released from the Purge's clutches. The heavy chain of failure garlanded his struggling heart, pinning him against the curved glass wall. He pulled upon it, his broken teeth grinding in his cracked jaw as he rallied against the pain. Muscles moved sluggishly beneath his skin, each crowding forward to lodge a complaint with his overworked and over-exerted brain. His internal organs sulked sullenly beneath them, casting mournful glances at each other as they took it in turns to shut down.

The sounds of his Shoal echoed in his ears, calling to him from distant waters. He had failed them. He cried aloud, a wordless expression of anguish. The Purge had taken them from him, his family, his people, his Shoal. Now he lay defeated, The Great Gollollopp, a broken and useless thing. All his scale-bound strength, all his piscine power was worthless before the fetid force of that unstoppable monster.

He called to the girl again, not knowing whether or not she was already lost.

The girl, too, he had failed; the creature of a thousand lives. Another life he had been unable to protect, to shield from the Purge's relentless hunger. Despite his best efforts, The Great Gollollopp had really dropped a clanger with this one. He tried to rise again, scraping forwards through the layers of grey sludge that swaddled him. His eyes creaked forwards, peering into the swimming shadows for something, *anything* that would indicate she was still alive.

There! Against the darkness something bright flashed a timid signal, a rebellious point of light shining in the oppressive gloom.

The Shoal called to him now, urging him to ignore the mysterious messenger.

Siren songs of the dead, echoes from the far blue danced a mournful jig around him; calling, imploring him to accept the darkness, to join them in the abyss. Heavy thoughts shuffled ponderously through his battered brain, lethargic from fighting against the pain that rolled endlessly through his ruined body. His thick lips, the bloody barracks that housed a regiment of broken teeth, parted slowly. Unconsciously they mouthed the names of his loved ones lost. Tears would have been welling, if he possessed the ducts for them to well from.

"Gollollopp!" The word rang clear, a familiar voice calling above the terminal melody that fell across him like a shroud. The point of light had moved, darting here and there. It glinted like a distant star as it cruised along the weak current. He flexed his gills, dragging at the scummy dregs of tainted water to send a brief flash of precious oxygen to his flagging mind.

The voice whispered straight into his mind, wriggling under his scales to bypass the dying ear completely. His plated eye swivelled in its hooded socket as the luminous pixie flitted out of the darkness. It hovered for a second or two, glowing just above the tip of his snout. He sniffed at it.

The mote blossomed in response, sending rays of light tickling across the layers of black and white scales that armoured his head. "Gollollopp!" It span cheerfully in place as it said his name, flaring hopefully. He sniffed again, "Meris?"

The little mote flared brighter, absorbing the word that fell from his panting lips. It looked at him quizzically – well, as much as a point of living light can – then, with a crack of lightning, burned itself into his flesh.

–::–

Deep within her chamber of petrified tissue, hounded and howled at by an unspeakable monstrosity, Meris sensed the faintest flutter of consciousness. She turned her attention towards it, pushing through the pain that consumed her. The Purge's teeth gnawed at her flesh while its thoughts burned like ice into her soul. It moved around her in an endless dance, its slithering sides rolling into a wall of amorphous darkness.

She flexed her fingers - or, at least, she imagined she did. A trickle of warmth, some hidden memories, flowered across her arm. Her breath quivered in her chest, her mind bound by droning agony. She drew herself into a knot, desperately trying to dampen the merciless coils of pain that lashed her. Somewhere out there, a part of her had escaped the onslaught; was a tiny survivor that hid within something old, something powerful, something that bristled with rage. "Where are you?" she whispered.

The Purge rose up before her, fanning out a cobra's hood as the girl twitched, her mind still trying to pull away. It swallowed, a thick bulge travelling down its swollen throat. "Ah, little sister, you do surprise me." It dipped forwards, the mismatched grin dripping before her, "It seems there is some fight in you left yet; I am impressed. Now, tell me... What is your secret, hmm? What are you up to?"

Heat bloomed in her breast. She blew out gently, calming herself, slowing her heartbeats. The pain and the cold became a part of her, a constant presence that dogged her every thought and movement. A plume of fire sprouted from her greying body, flaring at the creature.

The Purge hissed, recoiling briefly as another flurry of flames leapt from her skin. "What is this, sister? What have you hidden from me?" It asked, eyeing her malevolently as it snapped its jaws above her head.

Meris remained silent, her thoughts focused on the water, on the current that brushed against her skin. She

111

felt the rustling plants that struggled beneath her, the effervescence that swirled from the opening of a nearby pipe, and a tired mind that hovered on the edge of death.

She smiled, transplanting her mind from the body the Purge held and focusing on the minute mote that burned inside the fallen warrior. Her eyes opened, the violet points within them flickering amid a corona of starlight.

Gollollopp inhaled deeply as life itself flowed through his veins, reviving and regenerating as it went. He puffed out his gills as his muscles swelled with renewed strength. The fish rose from the silt, growling as his vision cleared. Golden light surrounded him, dancing a warm aurora across his armoured sides. Old wounds knitted, bones clicking back into place. Before him the cylindrical world expanded, opening out into a terrible tableau.

The girl that once shone with such a brilliant incandescence had been reduced to a wretched, broken thing in the creature's grip. Dying embers dripped from her wounds as the Purge snapped its vile jaws about her, its flapping coils looped around her. Its elongated head bowed, drinking in the curling flames and guttering ethereal tendrils that rippled out from the heart of the furnace.

It was killing her.

Something stirred in the Great Gollollopp's mind, a tiny voice that stripped him of his pain and lifted his heart from the deep well of despair that had held it. Fire filled his veins, as rage and bloodlust drowned his thoughts. His teeth bared as he charged forwards, leaping from the silt on powerful fins. His mouth opened in a primal roar, his mind burning with vengeance.

The Purge turned its head lazily, the face stretching and distorting as its focus shifted. The world shook with sound as the fish barrelled through the red-tinted water.

The Great Gollollopp's scales shone crimson, his once-white flanks standing out against his black markings like molten iron; he was a fishy phoenix, brimming with renewed life and well-fermented righteous fury.

The Purge screamed a challenge; a rage-fuelled roar that shifted in pitch as the fish thundered down the glass tube.

In its grip, Meris exploded back into life; the break from the creature's onslaught allowing her to release what little energy she had hidden from it. An eruption of orange fire rushed from her; pure, untainted chemical life-force that caught it by surprise, pushing the beast backwards.

Its face melted where the light struck it, oozing flesh dripping from its nightmarish bones to reveal the disfigured skull beneath. The skeleton glistened gunmetal grey before shifting into new and – if conceivably possible – even more horrifying positions. The Purge's face would have been difficult for even the most devoted of mothers to love, but its new fizzog was a trial too far. The black mass clicked and clacked as it slithered across its new skull. A collection of snapping jaws distended in a mass of barbed mandibles and thrashing tentacles.

The Purge faltered for a split second, its attention torn between the crimson fish that roared towards it and the solar flare that burned in its grasp. It struck outwards, shielding itself from the fish behind a forest of scrabbling spines while its loathsome body tightened to crush the girl's physical form.

Meris took her chance and dissolved, her human form splintering into a million gold-and-black striped fish that shot out in all directions. The rows of spears that sprouted from its body clashed together, twisting and turning as fireworks of glistening bodies melted around it. She skipped over the Purge's horned snout as it snapped forwards, the rows of teeth slamming into the empty space Meris occupied only moments before. Those wicked limbs struck out after her, a snatching, slashing mess of terrible talons that rushed through the water.

Meris had gambled well; her shoal of plucky runaways flowed around the Purge's colossal clutches, leaving the thing flailing at nothing but empty water. It screamed at her, snapping and thrashing at the tiny fish that danced around it. The spines contracted as it shifted form, its limbs becoming jaws and fins and claws that chased her through the murk. Its bloodlust consumed it, predatory desire overwhelming its wicked mind.

Thus, the Purge was suitably distracted when the Great Gollollopp, the Red-tinted Avenger, entered the fray. He tore past her, scattering the fleeing shoal. "Flee!" he bellowed the command. The hundred fish heads of Meris nodded in obedience. She swarmed together, her tiny fins sending her diamond-shaped bodies spinning and reeling away from the gods of war.

There was a wet smack - the only kind of smack possible underwater - as Fish met Purge in a collision of truly titanic proportions. The shockwave rolled through the water, buoying her escape as it propelled her down the glass tunnel. Countless eyes, varying in shades of blue and green, turned to watch as her red-tipped fins wriggled through the water.

The Great Gollollopp tore at the thrashing Purge. A sound exactly like - but in essence, utterly different from - lightning hitting a vat of treacle filled the water as the raging fish ripped great ugly lumps of blackness from its foe's gargantuan and rather repulsive body. Above it, two twitching limbs melded together into a vicious scimitar that swung down from the shadows. Empowered by Meris' gift, the Great Gollollopp dodged; twisting away from the blow, leaving behind only a few scattered scales that sparkled like rubies.

He dived again; parrying back a flurry of sabre blows with his muscle-bound tail. The Purge hissed, eyes and mouths opening and closing along the entirety of its shifting form. It slunk downwards before rising to tear at the fish's wide underbelly. Gollollopp dodged again, executing a perfect barrel roll as the beast surged past him. He rammed it two, three times, ignoring the scrabbling barbs that lodged in his iron-clad snout.

Meris' shoal stretched, her consciousness torn between the climactic battle and the relative safety of the shrouded spigot. Little fish darted back and forth amongst the shoal, her own sense of preservation fighting her curiosity to make good their escape.

A fat tentacle thrashed in the Great Gollollopp's jaws, writhing and stinging as he clamped it between his teeth. A shake of his head tore it free from the toxic mass and sent it spiralling into the silt, where it snarled and twitched with a life of its own.

The Purge coiled around him, lancing him with stingers and spines, its many teeth biting at the fish's armoured back. The Great Gollollopp weathered the pain, his body stronger than ever. He ignored the blood that flowed in the water like battle standards from a spider's web of open wounds. Undaunted by the Purge's furious assault, he gave as good as he got, trading blow for brutal blow with his pestilent foe.

Tiny mouths called words of encouragement, spitting strands of restorative nutrients to where her champion duelled. They splashed across his flank like golden raindrops on barren earth, the wounded flesh knitting together as it drank them eagerly. The knot of fish grew as more of the escaping shoal hung back to offer their support. A straining line of glistening bodies formed a swaying chain between them and the riveted brass gate. Hope once more beat in a hundred miniature hearts. One by one her bodies moved forward, the desire to save the Great Gollollopp rising above her fear of the Purge. *She would help him*. Meris had seen within the creatures mind, she would not fail him as she failed Scara.

As one she swam forwards, trailing light behind her like pollen.

Adrenaline fizzed in the Great Gollollopp's body, bolstering the bloodlust that powered his muscles. The valiant fish wanted nothing more than to kick this demon of detritus in the goolies harder than any goolies had ever been kicked before. The small matter of him lacking feet with which to kick, and that the monster he intended to give a kicking to lacked the required goolies, did nothing to dissuade him.

The Purge raked its claws across his back. He shrugged off the pain; it was of little consequence to him. He would not survive this battle, he was no fool. Even with the girl's gift surging through him, he was outmatched. At best he would mortally wound it, if such a thing could be wounded in such a way; hopefully wounded in some form of goolie, and leave this world knowing the murderer of the Infinite Shoal would die a slow and painful death. He would be waiting for it in oblivion, ready to fight it forever through the endless seas of eternity. His satisfied smile, filled with foul tasting anti-flesh, faded as the first waves of warmth caressed his side.

A great eye, a strong and noble eye built of blue-tinted fish-glass turned on the smattering of tiny fish that struggled in the wake of his movements. Surprise and anger lit the disc, glowering across its angular plates. "No!" he cried aloud, rage and exhaustion tipping his words as he dived beneath an unidentifiable limb; all horns and claws and twitching muscles. "No, Meris you must flee! Do not let it catch you again. Flee, now, flee!"

Too late, she had realised her error. The Purge slammed down with all its weight, driving lances deep within the Great Gollollopp's body. He cried out in agony, his words still commanding her to escape.

The Purge laughed as it sent a web of tendrils towards her, each one tipped with a hook that clawed at the water. "Come to me, little sister." it sneered, "Come and watch your warrior die!"

Horror gripped her, *what had she done?* A trail of bubbles burst from her as once again she scattered, sending what motes of restorative energy she could into the wounds of her great protector. His bulk shifted as he moved to shield her from the creature, his injuries glowing here and there as they tried to repair. "Go!" he grunted, forcing the Purge's blades from his haunches.

The word rode the waves around her as she darted through the brine, snapping at her fins and driving her forwards like hounds behind a flock of scaly sheep. The shoal reformed, a golden cloud shimmering through the water. She looked back as she swam - how could she not?

She saw those old, paternal eyes track her progress; the last creeping trails of golden light that tended his wounds, those fanning fins paddling back and forth. His crest rose, a sheer sail above his mottled flank, burning bright in the red glow like a mountain at sunrise. His throat shook as his battle cry filled the water, his bulk turning to face his foe.

She watched, too, as the Purge expanded before him, the fell creature once more an amorphous blob of shadowy stuff that would be deemed too unsavoury for most nightmares. The current in the tube slowed as it grew to fill the channel, its back growing a thick plated shell heavy with bristles and spines like that of a bloated lobster. She screamed as a tear opened in its sagging stomach. Fangs emerged, dripping with all sorts of slime and other such venomous muck, from lips gaping wide to reveal a putrid pink mass of forked tongues that rippled and writhed in utterly repellent ways. It lurched forwards, flopping heavily on rolls of ribbed fat as the Great Gollollopp charged, light flowing from his shining red armour like the robes of a king, the ethereal wings of an archangel. His bellowing roar, the war cry of The Great Gollollopp, Lord of the Infinite Shoal and Warden of the Eastern Trenches, dominated the world as he struck the very heart of the beast.

From the Purge came a scream, and a hiss, and then the clattering sound of too many mismatched teeth slamming together in a very final sort of way.

Silence followed, the silence of a thousand voices cut short. Meris didn't hear her own sob of despair as the vast shade closed its mouth around the piscine warrior. His thrashing shape showed within it for a split second; his noble form silhouetted against the shifting, squirming blob for a last, brief, painful second before the beast collapsed inwards.

Time took a leaf out of sound's book and also took a breather.

The nightmare loomed, vile and bulbous in victory. Foul and frozen, it pushed against the curving confines of brass and glass. The silt hovered nervously, unsure of where it needed to be in the tableaux while red light trickled through the water with an 'I told you so' smugness. The whole moment teetered on the brink of activity, reeling in the passing of a great and majestic creature.

Everything and nothing fought in the power vacuum, vying to be the first to happen. Everything turned out to be a dirty fighter and left nothing curled up in a corner, grabbing time roughly by the shoulders and dragging it back into life.

Things happened - not particularly *good* things, but things all the same.

The Purge surged forwards, rolling and churning like a bank of heavy storm clouds. Across its mottled back mouths and eyes, and things that could have had a fair whack at being either, sprouted and burst like hate-filled buboes.

The pipe shook as the thing stretched and slammed against it. From its sides a whirling, whipping forest of limbs pulled it forwards, oozing itself towards the golden constellation of diamond-shaped fish. Teeth and lips screeched and sucked, hissing her name, salivating over each syllable as it dragged itself along the pipe.

The striped shoal that was Meris bunched for a second, melting into a twirling knot of shining bodies that looped and threaded within it. Long fronds of greenery coiled around her, hiding in the huddle of rusting pipes that cowered in the corner of the section.

A hundred eyes twisted and turned, her stomachs churning as its scent encroached further in her nostrils. The memory of its barbed talons still scratched at the edge of her mind, grey scars shading her thoughts with a faint cross hatch. Red-tipped fins pumped furiously, tiny teeth ground together. A percussion orchestra of hearts thumped in a singular rhythm as the Purge rose up before her, its shifting limbs outstretched to snatch her from the water.

It grinned, and Meris fled.

The Purge's motley collection of multi-species eyes widened with hateful surprise as its prey dissolved amongst the pale green boscage of billowing fronds.

Howls of rage sounded from the throats on its shoulders, the mouths in its stomach bellowing in unison. The world filled with darkness as it pounced, limbs scratching at the glass, ripping the plants from their sediment beds. They wilted at its touch, ignored as they turned into more grey dust.

The great bulk of nightmares swept over and beyond the rusted brass valve, slamming into it with a reverberating clang. The valve bent under its abominable weight, folding around itself as a ton of anti-flesh fought to crawl inside of it. The Purge twisted and thrashed as its body corkscrewed through the misused portal. It slithered after her in a vicious viscous form, a vile vision of bloodshot eyes and multipurpose orifices that pursued her in a foully fluid motion.

Meris didn't look back as she surged through the lightless interior of the brass pipe. The metal walls around her shook as the Purge threw its weight against it, screaming as it forced itself through the restrictive space. She was a thing of speed now, her body fusing into that of a whiskered loach, a streamlined fish perfectly suited to navigate the twisting labyrinth ahead. Oxygen filled her gills as she raced ahead, her muscles and fins paddling harder than ever before in honour of those that had sacrificed so much to keep her alive.

Whatever it was she was here to do, she would do it for them; for the man Scara and the Great Gollollopp, and the countless other lives that had already been lost. She swam ever downwards, determined to find the light.

The chase, it could be argued, was on.

The last few days have been difficult for all of us, though none more so than Porvine. He has been withdrawn and melancholic. Considering his position and his closeness to the project, this was to be expected. Still, I have ordered him to be watched with increased vigilance.

In his absence, I have assumed full command of the Institute and all staff held within. My new appointment was met with no resistance.

McClusky volunteered to take over the daily running of the Institute, allowing me to focus my efforts on more pressing matters. She is highly capable and commands the respect of her staff; I am fortunate to have her as an ally.

On my orders the Purge has been ceased and destroyed.

*The birthing chambers are being drained, and the extracted water cleansed by evaporation at high temperature.
A number of SyMons have been repurposed to scour the system for any remaining traces. Their technicians are under instruction to seal and sterilise any section of the Network that shows signs of infection.*

We cannot allow that Thing to manifest again.

It is clear to me that what we hold here is a chemical weapon greater than anything the Earth has seen before. Though any aggressor would come for the MERIS technology, the Purge is a far greater asset to those who would end this war through bloodshed.

To ensure its security, all data pertaining to the Purge has been confined to a single info-key and the activation protocol held within the Citadel's disused auxiliary matrix.

I shall think hard on how to keep the key from our enemies.

—::—

I have now accepted our isolation.

Despite McClusky's best efforts, our communications receive no reply. It is her opinion that either Command has fallen, or our signals are being blocked by unknown forces. Though her team have been unable to restart our automated defence systems, she has found some data worthy of note.

There are reports on the initial requisition of advanced battle cogs, droids developed in the earlier days of the Institute as part of an automated security force. Details are few, though three letters link them: ODP. A manual search of the complex has returned no results.

This news does not dismay me; it is likely they would have been no more useful than the ones we used on the field.

Her orders are to investigate further, but to retain focus on the parts of the defence network we can see: the camera and sentry turrets. So far, they have remained unresponsive. Whatever encryption her predecessor sealed them with has proven unbreakable.

I have informed the guard of our situation; it is no longer worth keeping them from the truth. They have doubled their drills, and a number of the stewards and technicians have been drafted to bolster our remaining forces.

It is only a matter of time until we see war upon our island. When it comes, we shall fight them alone.

Chapter Ten

AS Meris descended the myriad levels of the once-proud Institute, navigating the network of brass pipes with the Purge in hot and horrid pursuit, something else happened.

Specifically, that something was the turning-on of a light. It was a little, unremarkable blue light that clung to the side of one of those brass pipes; a little blue light that blinked on and off, on and off, on and off. It illuminated the concrete shaft through which the pipes passed, bouncing off the grey walls to settle on long lost cobwebs and dust-covered plumbing.

Now usually, there's nothing overly suspicious about a little light turning on - usually. In this case, taking into account the fact that the light in question only started blinking once Meris had passed its lonely station, perhaps you have cause to raise an eyebrow. Well, eyebrow raised or not, that little light marked the girl's passage in a very curious way indeed.

Its little sensors, attached to a nest of fiddly wires, sent an electronic message to the microcomputer ensconced nearby. There was a bit of binary deduction on the microcomputer's part, followed by a spot of serious silicon scrutiny.

A beep may have been beeped, but if it had been, it failed to stand out amongst the general dripping of drips and hissing of steam that comprised the majority of the shaft's acoustic activity. The computer equivalent of muttering and head-nodding happened, and a message was beamed up and away through the crumbling honeycomb of steel and stone.

It mucked about for a bit; looping around exposed steel girders, mooching over the corpses of ruined machines and generally taking its sweet, synthetic time to get from A to B. The message eventually found its way to a lonely tower at the very edge of the Institute and skulked into the small, circular room that crowned it.

The message bunched its shoulders and looked around in a shifty way, expecting any second to be admonished for not visiting more often.

The two inhabitants of the windowless cell paid it no heed. With no admonishment forthcoming, the message wiped a greasy brow with the back of its metaphorical sleeve and dropped heavily into a dusty receiving dish.

It swirled around the sides for a bit, the codes daring each other to take the plunge, before disappearing into another tangle of wires and technogubbins. The whole exchange, from beeping pipe light to lofty control room receiver took almost three quarters of a second which, to be fair, isn't bad when you consider the state of the place.

The message, now received, set all manner of things in motion.

A yellowing Bakelite console ran around the perimeter of the room, sloping upwards from the octagonal operating area. Its surface was festooned with knobs and buttons and switches and levers that lurked beneath a sombre stratum of settled soot. A reluctant fan whirred into life somewhere below it all, grinding and moaning as it wafted slightly cooler air over slowly warming computer bits. Here and there, sounds like '*glurk*' and '*by-erk*' and '*whuzzit*' huffed about in an almost-productive manner.

A whole bank of blue lights waved at each other, illuminating in an ever-changing pattern that winked and blinked in the gloom.

Two such lights, bigger and rounder than their desktop-bound brethren, shone out from the smooth and featureless face of a System Monitoring Droid, more commonly dubbed 'SyMon', who had been woken by the process.

SyMon blinked, the lights that gave the impression of eyes shutting off and then back on again with little '*plink plink*' noises. There was a whirring of old motors as he rose from where he had lain slumped and inactive across the dusty dials and grubby gadgets.

"Mwerp?" he asked to the room at large.

More lights scuttled around the console like beetles, clustering around incoming morsels of data before clicking away through the dust. SyMon arched his copper-plated back, his gears grinding and wires sparking as he did so. He made the typical groaning you'd associate with the motion, albeit with a distinct electronic twang. A scuffle of dust was shrugged from his skinny shoulders as he stretched out a pair of wiry arms. His quadruple-jointed fingers interlinked together as he cracked his knuckles, proffering a popping sound to punctuate the wheezing and snickering of the various rousing gadgets and gizmos.

SyMon leaned forwards, peering pensively into a bowed bunch of buzzing screens. A surprising message stood out against the grey green background. A message so surprising, it almost carved eyebrows into his smooth face plate and raised them - almost. If it had been successful in carving those eyebrows, they would have quickly furrowed into an irritated scowl.

[POSITIVE DETECTION]; what nonsense. A metal fist was brought down heavily upon the truculent telescreen in the time- old manner of dealing with malfunctioning machines.

The message fizzled and died as the console sulked, and then reluctantly rebooted. SyMon's fingers flew across keypads and consoles, twiddling toggles and flipping switches. The message swaggered onto the screen again, jeering at the robot.

[POSITIVE DETECTION] slouched against the screen. SyMon watched with house-proud indignation as the message continued; [POSITIVE DETECTION – LEVEL EIGHTEEN]. He mimed holding his breath as a little green block flashed, waiting patiently as the system double and triple checked itself. Blink blink; held breath, held breath.

[CONFIRMED]

SyMon's designers really should have added a jaw to his face. The robot desperately needed something to drop as the word, a brave statement, shone out from the screen.

[POSITIVE DETECTION – LEVEL SEVENTEEN – CONFIRMED] followed. His head flitted like a bird, twitching from screen to screen to screen. Level sixteen, fifteen, fourteen; a countdown filled every monitor. [CONFIRMED – CONFIRMED – CONFIRMED].

He leaned backwards. The wheels that supported his titanium torso squeaked out a plea for a spot of oil. The automaton turned in place, trundling sideways along tracks set into the floor. He bobbed as he went, rocking gently on his hydraulic supports to where his human colleague snoozed against the closed door.

SyMon winced as a particularly loud squeal leaked out of his wheels and threatened to rouse the sleeper. He shushed it with a wave and slowed his approach. He drew near, then nearer still, creaking quietly like a galleon in a library.

"Psszt," he whispered, gently nudging his comatose colleague's booted foot.

His colleague, a young technician by the name of Tamik, remained still. His mouth hung ever so slightly open, the lips dry and pulled tight. His head drooped heavily upon his chest.

In the response department, he was definitely lacking.

"Psszt," he repeated, slightly louder this time, "Tamzik, psszt Tamzik, wvake up."

SyMon shook his colleague with added vigour. The young man's loose bootlaces flopped wildly like the wings of a startled bird. His arm, which had lain heavily across his blue-suited chest, slipped forwards to reveal a brown rose of dried blood. There was a small, cold thud as his lifeless hand settled amongst the drifts of dust.

SyMon took in the grisly sight and tutted, as only a vaguely-anthropomorphic robot can.

Tamik had been told times many to keep his uniform clean and correct. The young man would be annoyed that he had slept through such a momentous occasion, and while SyMon really wished he could have had a second opinion, nobody could say he hadn't tried to rouse the tatty technician.

He considered requesting the opinion of a supervisor, a consideration that lasted a deep and thoughtful nanosecond, before deciding against it. He certainly didn't want to get his good friend Tamik in trouble, and besides, they were probably busy preparing for the activation.

It was probably best not to disturb them.

SyMon shook Tamik's boot a final time, before taking matters into his own human-like hands. There was a faint hiss and a whine as his hydraulic supports extended him forwards. He dangled precariously over his dozing chum, the supports fully stretched and struggling to hold his outstretched weight. Carefully, he unbuttoned Tamik's breast pocket, rubbing a dark red smut from an otherwise shiny gold button as he did so.

He rummaged briefly, adding the ability to stick out a thoughtful tongue to the growing list of upgrades he would request at the earliest opportunity.

A small pleather pouch was produced and lifted carefully away; his clockwork arm clicking as it retracted. Tamik remained still. A very sound sleeper, reasoned SyMon. He patted his friend affectionately on his padded shoulder before turning on his axis and trundling back to his station.

He would be sure to tell Tamik all about it when he woke up.

Deft fingers withdrew a silver key from the slightly worn pouch. The weak, yellow light caught it; playing across the curves and contours of the flowers that had been lovingly and mechanically carved into its handle.

SyMon held it reverently in both hands, a sacred item.

His smooth head bowed ever so slightly, his lamplike eyes glowing reverently. The track conveyed the robot to where an eight-spoked wheel sat patiently atop a copper-bound column. Cobwebs and wires fought for space up and down its sides, trailing off into shadowy recesses and softly humming machines.

A vent appeared in its domed centre as he approached, lit by a polite light.

SyMon's head swung this way and that as he pondered whether to continue on this course of action. Protocol did state that only a human should activate this part of the system, and there was little he loved more than following protocol. On the other diode, he was helping out a colleague and going the extra mile, something his personnel programs certainly promoted. He nodded to the room at large and entered the key into the waiting lock.

A klaxon rang from the machine, like the cheering of a harp at a football match.

SyMon threw himself forwards with gear driven gusto, grabbing the handles and turning them with his formidable robot strength. Around him messages whizzed and whooped through the air, waking distant machines and rallying long-dormant programs.

All across the Institute, little blue lights winked in the darkness.

He beamed happily as he worked; it was time to wake up.

DATA TRANSCRIBED FROM THE VIDI-LOG OF:
Captain Horatio Scara

DATA RETRIEVED FROM [CLASSIFIED], STATUS: NON-OPERATIONAL

DATA RETRIEVAL DATE: [CLASSIFIED]

We have made discoveries both great and grave.

Internal:

In the ruins of the birthing chamber, a single subject survived.

It is small and stunted, compared to the others. Despite this, it holds the regeneration matrix in an almost-stable state. It appears it did not activate with its brothers and sisters, and remains unconscious within its pod.

There has been much speculation as to why it was overlooked by the Purge. I cannot explain why or how it survived; it is a miracle.

I have granted Porvine permission to remotely extract and relocate the specimen to a secondary chamber. Its body is weak, and damaged by the failed activation. Despite this, he believes he can create a clone from it.

He is a man of rejuvenated faith. He must work quickly, as his time is limited.

McClusky has reported an anomaly. When the subject was removed from the pod, a number of systems activated briefly before shutting down. This is encouraging; it appears that her predecessor has linked our defence systems into the MERIS life-support. She is working tirelessly, though the system is unfamiliar to her.

With the Purge eradicated and contained, I have ordered the SyMons to be programmed to assist her team.

Privately, I have expressed my admiration of the dedication she has to her duty, and the interaction has left us on more familiar terms.

When not in the company of our subordinates, she has taken to calling me Horatio.

I have taken to calling her Bos.

The subject of our meetings shall not be held on file.

External:

The enemy has been spotted moving en-mass towards the island. The vanguard of their landing ships flies the ragged red standards of the Mother's Men. We do not have the fliers to assault them at range, and what few exterior guns can be operated manually have limited ammunition.

We are fortunate that those who built this place centuries before our arrival had planned for war. The walls are sextuple-layered concrete, reinforced with steel supports. The main doors are arguably as strong and can be deadlocked, requiring either electronic override by senior command, or an unthinkable force from within.

I have already ordered that all other entrances be sealed, and the external shutters lowered.

To maintain morale and wellbeing, we will move into a system of daily Changes: replicated 'Day' and 'Night' modes displayed upon regularly-spaced monitor screens. This will simulate time passing as normal, and keep the population from idling on the forces gathering at our gates.

Our stores are not what they could be, but if carefully rationed should be sufficient to keep us alive long enough to break the siege.

With all nonessential work conscripted to Porvine's clone

project, McClusky's tech team, or our defence, progress is being made in leaps and bounds.

They will make landfall tomorrow; they will find us ready, and impregnable.

Though it does not do to be over confident, I look forward to seeing them break upon our walls.

We will prevail.

Chapter Eleven

MERIS twisted and turned, shifting from form to form as she descended through the many levels of the labyrinthine network. The Purge roared and crashed behind her, nipping at her fins as it tore through the pipes fierce pursuit.

A scurry of chocolate brown fish burst from a tapered vent, tails flapping wildly as they corkscrewed together. The shoal merged fluidly into a powerful coarse fish, with silver-green scales and sharp yellow fins. Free from the confines of the pipe for now, Meris made the most of her larger, stronger form to race ahead of the following Purge.

She sped along empty canals, leaping from waterfalls and diving through plunging tunnels until at last the rage-fuelled screams of the Purge drifted from hearing. Meris slowed just slightly, paddling through a maze of glass tunnels that looped between the catacombs of empty laboratories. She descended through a brass inlet, slicing through the current like a knife. The course turned, curving downwards to a vent, heavy with algae, which sought to bar her progress.

Her form split again into the shivering shoal, flowing through the gaps and out into a wide, half-lit space. Her bodies flowed together, becoming the girl once more, and she stole a moment of rest.

Around her, the wide glass walls curved and bowed; obscured by a rippling current that flowed from a series of cleverly concealed impellers. The world beyond was swathed in shadow, leaving nothing but the blurred suggestions of mechanical shapes backlit by the occasional ominous red light.

This part of the Network was the residence of a consortium of jellyfish, a forest of whom drifted upwards to receive her. What little light penetrated the thick glass walls shone upon their pale bodies, painting them with warm summer hues of pinks and oranges that glowed like embers against the ambient blue of the deep water beneath them. They hummed to each other as they drifted upwards, a gentle sound that undulated between the acoustic and the telepathic.

Meris' eyes flitted between them and the vent above her. Even now she could sense the Purge, feel it itching at the back of her mind. It drew closer with each passing second. She called out to the swarm, warning them of what pursued her. They rippled thoughtfully, siphoning her words through their pulsing bodies.

A single polyp broke away from the dancing crowd, to float before her nose. It lit up as it spoke to her.

"You," it sighed, its words echoed by its kin. "You were the one that was foretold."

"Did you not hear me?" She blinked, her hands steadying herself against the glass. "The Purge is coming, it will follow me here. I'm sorry, I'm so sorry, but you must flee. Do you understand?"

"Yes, we understand. You are the one that was, the one that would be." It hovered expectantly before her eyes.

"I don't- I don't know what that means..." She could sense the Purge growing closer; it would not be long before it found her again. "You must leave this place, something terrible is coming!"

The jellyfish dipped. "We cannot."

"But it will kill you – all of you. Please, you must go!" Meris's voice rose with panic, as she pleaded with the pulsating polyp. The swarm expanded and contracted, dancing within itself like a living kaleidoscope.

"You are the one that was, the one that would be." it repeated. A shiver went through the swarm as the words echoed through the water.

"I'm sorry, but I don't understand. I don't know what that means!" Tears pricked her eyes as ghosts of pain drifted through her. *How could she make them understand?* "Please!" she begged, "You cannot stay here! The Purge is coming it'll, it'll–"

A thunderclap silenced her. The world erupted in yellow light as the jellyfish's song grew louder. More and more of them rose from the depths to dance around her, their bodies forming intricate patterns in the water. The current parted, a circle opening in the crowd of flesh to reveal a single image. *Her* image.

Beyond the glass, her likeness filled an entire wall. Her painted violet eyes watched coldly, her arms outstretched as though ready to embrace her. The jellies swarmed into a living frame that twisted the light around them.

"You are what has always been, what will one day become." Their words warped the world around them, spinning their bodies through the current. "You are the one who carries us, the one who guides, the one who brings the light and draws the darkness; the one who births life and consumes death. You are the one who watches."

Any potential response on Meris's part was quashed by a rending scream from above. The sound vibrated harshly through the water, buffeting the bulbous jellyfish. The humming rose briefly, stinging her ears, before settling back into its endless mantra.

"The Purge! The Purge is coming!" she cried, "Please, come with me, please!"

"We cannot." the polyp spoke again, "we cannot leave this place. You are the one that takes us from here."

Meris's heart thrummed in her chest as she beat back her fear of the creature that howled in the distance. "I can't! I don't know how, please, just come with me!"

"You are the one that carries us from here." The polyp droned as it skipped away to join the swirling mass of its brethren, "You are the one that holds our memory, that takes our sacrifice and births us anew in distant waters. Find us, and take us to the light."

The jellyfish rose as one, lifting around her like angels ascending into the heavens. Their words had barely left her ears when the Purge exploded from the vent, shattering the algae-clad metal around it.

A phantasm of flailing limbs and howling mouths, the creature bled from one hideous shape to another as it slithered downwards. An ulcerous mound of red eyes framed a sucker-like mouth ringed by rows of needle-thin teeth. The filthy maw spread ever wider as it descended, peeling backwards as it inverted itself into a new and more terrible form.

It really was a horrid sight.

The jellyfish swam upward to meet it, their bodies compacting into a storm of translucent clouds, "Leave us now, Watcher. Leave us to the darkness, and raise us into the light. Remember us."

Meris nodded, diving down through the jungle of trailing tendrils.

The poison-tipped streamers brushed harmlessly across her scales as she pushed through the thickening mass. They flowed around her, an endless mass of bodies turning the world into a fog of shifting pastel shades; a polychromatic blizzard of wobbly, blobby bodies. They gathered close, a living protective shroud opening briefly to allow her passage before clustering back together in her wake.

Their humming filled her ears, the constant sound developing a razor edge of extrinsic medusozoan anger. Despite the words of sacrifice, there was no mistaking that the jellies had taken more than a little umbrage to having their sanctum invaded by the metamorphosing monstrosity.

Behind her they meshed together, their long tendrils interlocking to form a silvery web of electrified poison. Their domed heads blibbed and blobbed; vibrating as a single force of invertebrate intimidation.

The Purge snarled as it approached, a million mad eyes peering through the living mist in search of its prey. The wall expanded before it; spreading fleshy white wings like a vast, alien swan.

Meris felt the Purge strike the gathered jellies as she slipped into one of the circular outlets that dwelled at the base of their kingdom. The Purge roared above their chorus, ripping and thrashing downwards, their dying cries trailing after her.

Once again, she was in darkness, with the sounds of death tumbling in her wake.

She held them in her thoughts as her body compressed into a fluid mass of jostling fish, to better navigate the confined space. The shoal coiled within the maze of twisting pipes, pushing onward. The brass pipes convulsed, the strained metal groaning as the Purge squeezed into them. She coalesced, becoming a streamlined catfish that raced ahead of the baying creature that hounded her.

Light erupted briefly around her; the space widened, allowing her a few seconds to morph into a quintet of winged fish that leapt from the water to glide across the open canal before returning back to the darkness of the metal tunnels. Her eyes expanded, her form shifting from creature to creature as she swam blindly, draining what little light she could steal on her flight past portholes blurred by grime and smoke.

Beyond the glass, the grim lights in their round cages painted the endless hive of concrete labs and whitewashed corridors, disfigured and marred by the scars of war, bright with the shade of fresh blood. They flared, as if responding to the Purge. Their eruptions were harbingers, twisted pilot fish swimming before the gorging black chimera of hatred that chased her into the depths.

Here and there, hidden amongst the burning wreckage that drifted by like the ruins of sunken ships, tiny blue lights rebelled against the oppressive crimson regime. They winked from long-forgotten consoles and broken monitors, scuttling unseen down optical wires and relaying secret messages between technological conspirators. It was all very cloak and dagger, sans the physical cloaks and daggers.

This, Meris didn't see - not that it would have been apparent what was going on. Instead, more pressing matters came in the form of escaping the wrong 'un behind her.

"Sssister..." it called, its voice hissing through the tube, slithering around her. "Come to me, sisster..."

Its claws clicked as it chased her through the labyrinth, the water streaming past her as it sucked and wheezed. She pressed herself ever forward, fighting to resist its probing invitations.

For the second time in a Change, Meris was consumed by exhaustion. Without the pulsating screens, time was allowed to pass unchecked. Her journey was marked by her own fatigue, a growing demon that whispered temptations and gnawed at her muscles.

Though once again the speed of her flight had put space between her and her hunter, to stop, to rest, was certain death. Her nemesis pursued tirelessly, its taunts and cries a constant presence in her ears. She shifted forms slowly now, blending like watercolours across a tired and struggling spectrum of sea life.

And so, it was as a wavering line of gasping gobies that she entered the Great Hall. She didn't know it as the Great Hall, oh no. To Meris, the growing current and distant lights were a blessing, drawing her forth from the darkness.

Her fins fluttered at her sides, paddling in the water as the piscine procession tumbled over the edge of one of the waterfalls that fed into a wide semicircular pool. She descended the column of water safely, allowing the current to carry her to the edge of a stone-ringed bower, teeming with fish and bright with corals. She shifted again, her shoal of gobies waltzing wearily together until once again she drifted within her almost-human form.

The Purge would be in hot pursuit; this she was all too aware of, but for a few seconds she allowed herself to be cradled by the gently lapping waves. Emerging from the cliff face above her, an immaculately carved statue of Meris stared out across the high-vaulted hall with flawless marble eyes. Bright veins of glittering minerals shot through the towering rock, making the figure shine in the glow of the countless blue lights that dusted the distant ceiling.

Its arms were spread wide, reaching out with serene generosity towards any who would enter from the world outside. It stood proudly amongst a forest of stone plants teased by skilled artisans from the monolith, framed on either side by a cloak of crashing water as the falls cascaded around her.

Meris leaned against the smooth granite that ran in

a long, low ridge around the outside of the pool. Her equivalent of sleep called to her, bleeding through her flesh and drawing her into a more docile form. From where she rested against the rocks, branches of maroon coral spread out in awkward movements. Swirls of fish billowed about her like autumnal leaves, bright and brilliant beneath the waves.

Though the chemical devil still hunted her, for the first time since the flowers she felt at peace. Under the water the shoals drifted across her skin as the corals continued to surge around her, the ecosystem thriving at her presence. She allowed her eyes to close for a brief second as she savoured the gentle sensation of flourishing growth that crept over her.

Vague murmurs of light dappled across her body, illuminating the coral that caressed her skin. Mottled fingers of plum and mauve brushed delicately across her lips as the tender colonies of acropora wove a bassinet of branches around her. They fussed and fretted, the whole curving reef reaching towards her. Their roots sank into her flesh, nourishing her body with the fruits of their photosynthesis while fatigue and exertion were drawn from her like venom from a snakebite.

Meris dared to relax, basking in the reef's rejuvenating embrace. Her breathing slowed, her thoughts settled, the ethereal light that glowed from her skin pulsed with quiet contentment. The ghosts that haunted her receded into the shadows of her subconscious. Scara's pain, Gollollopp's bravery, the Jellies' sacrifice, the countless men and women who had made this monument to science their tomb, fell silent.

They were gone, lost to the darkness of time. She should allow herself to rest, to sleep. Meris yawned, her thoughts heavy and dulled by exhaustion. For a tiny, forbidden moment she was at peace.

No.

Her eyes snapped open as she burst through the cage of clustering corals. Purple branches danced a broken ballet in the water as she flowed forward, her human shape twisting amongst a veil of golden light. The rippling surface shattered before her, swirling into flocks of tiny whirlpools that gathered at her feet as she leapt from the depths to walk upon it. She tilted her chin upward, and looked straight into the noxious celebration of wickedness that served as the Purge's face.

It squatted upon the edge of one of the two waterfalls; its foulness coalesced into that of a bloated and pestilent toad that poisoned the shallows. Wide paws settled upon the statue's shoulder, slithering across the spray-dampened stone. Black effluence seeped from it, seeping across the silver grey surface of the carved granite.

It grinned widely, its tongue lolling across its round stomach. On its flanks, smaller mouths continued to whisper their malodorous melodies. As always those round, red eyes, burning and bulbous and now very much part-and-parcel of the Purge's persona, popped and spread across its pure jet skin.

"Ah, little sister, could I not tempt you to rest? Such a shame; your death would have been much less painful. Still, it'll be more fun this way." A hidden throat emerged from a fold of skin on the creature's back, chuckling as it spoke. It extended a claw to the statue's face, leaving a trail of black mucous in its wake, emulating tears as it dripped from the marble eyes. It purred obscenely as it stroked the symmetrical cheeks with a strangely perverse mix of adoration and disgust.

The Purge turned one half of its face to watch as the globules slide wetly down the statue's face, the layer of filth obscuring the stern beauty beneath. The other half contorted, leering down at the girl in the pool. "How fitting," it hissed, "for that mockery of life you possess to be extinguished in the same hall where the first fires of our existence were lit."

"Enough, monster!" Meris' voice rang out into the darkened expanse, echoing off of distant walls. She strode across the water, her eyes filled with violet fire. "Enough of your vile whispers and evil words, enough of your poison. I have seen all of you, Purge; you have shown me everything you are, and all you are is death!"

The abomination beamed down at her, its fat lips curling as it salivated at this high praise. Gobbets of drool dripped from between yellow fangs, splashing into the crystal waters below. "Indeed," it smirked, "and what a glorious thing that is to be."

Meris' fists shook, her body radiating anger as a physical presence that rippled across the water's surface, causing small waves to tumble against the enclosing stone wall. Beneath her, the fish swept to and fro as a single being, an undulating mass of rainbow bodies dancing above the coral reef.

"You don't understand. Death is *nothing*! You, *you're* nothing. Just emptiness - a hollow nothing that you try to fill with endless hunger and hatred. A vile poison, a perversion, a bloated monster that kills and consumes everything it touches, and for what? Do you even know *why*? Do *you* know why you kill? Why you leave every place you visit grey, and cold, and lifeless? Do you even know *why* you pursue me? Why you hate me with such a passion that it destroys every living thing it touches?"

The water frothed and boiled beneath her as she spoke, lifting her towards where the Purge squatted in a silence marred only by the continuous sucking hiss that seeped from its body. It quivered, seething atop its perch. Spray drifted about it, dampening its body and causing it to glisten like oil in the crepuscular light.

She drew level with the creature, unconsciously directing the water to bear her towards her noxious nemesis. "If you know this, Purge; if you know why we are here, why we are lost in this horrible ruined place, then tell me! Tell me why my face is on every wall, why all manner of creatures have fought and died to either save or destroy me? Please either tell me, or kill me, for when I am no more perhaps all of this wickedness will end, and leave this place in peace."

The Purge shifted, its eyes melting, mouths and nostrils scuttling and closing as it hunched forwards. From a mass of muscles it excreted a vaguely-reptilian head festooned with clicking entomic accessories. From this fresh hell it spoke, a motley collection of pink tongues lolling from its mismatched maw as it did so.

"Merisss," it sneered, its words twisting in mockery, "The MERIS, their great work, the precious vessel of their salvation. How many of you do you think they made? How many prototypes, how many failures? How many abominations did they make? How many sickly creatures screamed and tore themselves apart, their minds burning with madness? So many false gods, so many stunted monsters."

Fat mammalian molars slipped into view as its demented grimace spread wider. It laughed its harsh and horrid laugh, that rank chuckle that sent shivers up even the most courageous spines. "How many tortured lives fluttered briefly, writhing in agony before being sent back into darkness? How many died, Meris? How many were purged to allow you, their little messiah, to be born?"

Meris tasted the truth in its words.

Somewhere in the darkened recesses of her mind she could hear them, feel them; small pale faces, half-formed and mewling in the shadows. Cold and alone, crying out from their sterile, electric prisons. She remembered their pain, as fresh and clear as though it was her own.

"I'm sorry." Her voice was quiet. She reached out to them, the Purge forgotten. "It's not- I don't- I'm sorry..."

Standing atop her frothing pedestal of swirling water, she felt very small indeed. Her saffron hive mind buzzed, filling with long-dead voices. The Purge's words were as powerful as ever, luring her into despair. She walked among the clouds of her thoughts. A fin twitched; a hand closed about hers; machines whirred in the distance; the golden light grew. The statue wept before her, the Purge's filth still dripping from it.

"You're too late, little sister," the Purge hissed forwards, "always too late. And now you ask for peace? You shall have no peace, Meris; there is nothing left for you but pain and death. You shall have your reward, Meris. Come now – let us end this, and be purged!"

It struck forwards, its mishmash of maws closing around empty air. Meris dove sideways as the monster passed beside her. The fear and doubt it sowed within her bled across her skin, dripping grey into the water that swayed beneath.

Her body rallied, golden light rushing through her limbs as they set about their task. She would run from this thing no more. It would not take her; it would not succeed in reducing the sacrifices of so many to naught.

She melted, becoming one with the writhing coil of water and folding it around her, the instincts that had for so long been suppressed now acting freely. The Purge hissed, scuttling across the statue on a multitude of legs. Its long, serpentine head struck out again; a forest of feelers and tentacles and all manner of appendages sprouting from its flesh to thrash wildly.

Meris was ready, and met it with tempestuous fury,

her voice crying out in wordless rage. A plume of water erupted forward, arching like a thrown fist to slam the creature against the stone. It shrieked and thrashed as the torrent ground it against the grey rock. It changed form, exploding into a swarm of crab-like monstrosities that clung to the moist surface. Another flurry of strikes fell upon them, smiting them until they were well and truly smote, their bodies crashing and breaking upon the rocks. They twitched obscenely as the torrent lessened, then broke into a falling mist that crafted pale rainbows from the weak light.

The girl reformed, diving gracefully from the collapsing waterspout and into the pool below.

A single thought shot out from her like a physical wave, rippling through the water as she disappeared beneath the surface. The command struck the citizens of the reef, instructing them to escape into the outlets that dotted the base of the pool.

They did as they were bid, forming a multiheaded and multicoloured mass that poured into the safety of the pipes below. The coral strained at their roots, trying as best they could to follow her orders. They would be added to the growing list of those who she could not save.

Something fell into the water behind her, the first of many similar somethings that plinked across the settling surface like the first drops of a rancid rain. Meris turned, her attention drawn to the small black blobs that fumbled in the gentle current like an ink made of nightmares.

A small fish snuck out of the reef, a straggler swimming behind the tail of the exodus below. Its little green eyes twitched, regarding the girl briefly before turning away from its fleeing fellows. A deep purple flag flew from its high dorsal fin, twitching as it swam, vivid against its yellow body. The fish wriggled up to the obscene blob, sniffing with an elongated nose.

The word "No!" barely had time to form between her lips, and the following exclamation mark didn't get a look in. The effect on the flag-waving fish, sadly, was instantaneous. A vile spider web struck out, draining first the colour, then the life, and then the flesh from the poor wee fishie. A shrivelled husk, a stained shred of spine, was all that remained to settle upon the white coral sand below.

Horror made itself known on the face of Meris.

The sporadic splatter of splashes surged into a doom-laden drumming as the billowing blobs exploded around her, dripping from the statue with vulgar menace. Meris backpedalled frantically as they drifted towards her, their vicious tendrils striking and snaring anything unfortunate enough to fall within their reach. To her left, fatty lumps of deadly darkness clustered together, raking at the once-thriving reef with snarling tentacles.

Meris felt the stone wall push firm against her back, grazing her skin, halting her retreat. Before her the pool was a mass of writhing evil, toxic waves slapping wetly against each other as coils of filth curled across the blue.

Her fingers found purchase against the curving stone, gripping its smooth contours. She rushed to the surface, breaking free as the darkness closed in around her. A single, fluid motion pulled her free of the water and onto the enclosing wall. She gasped aloud as lungs inflated in her chest. Her body ached as they devoured the air around her, trembling as it struggled to adapt without the support of the water.

Terra firma held no sympathy for the child of the waters.

She rose from her supine position, her bones and muscles strengthening to better serve on the land. Meris leapt, catlike, as tendrils of darkness whipped at her, striking the stones where she had lain but a second before.

The Purge filled the pool wholly now, its form larger than ever. Red eyes boiled over the water's surface, clustering like scum on a stagnant pond. It hissed as it pushed a lumpy and misshapen head forth.

A hundred tentacles sprouted from its back, flailing forwards to scrabble at the stone wall with claw-tipped suckers. Meris dodged them, her agility increasing as her confidence in the new form grew. They followed her as she ran along the wall's length, hissing and snapping at her heels.

The Purge roared, throwing another barrage of limbs towards her. Meris dodged, too slowly, and cried out as a coil whipped a line of golden blood across her back. The force of the blow lifted her off her feet, pitching from the wall and sending her crashing onto the hard marble tiles beyond. She rolled as she landed, steam rising from her back as she burned the Purge's venom from her wounds.

Meris pushed herself across the tiles crawling across the stone and drawing herself out of the Purge's reach. She sat panting as her injured flesh healed, her tunic sealing the tears across it.

Within the confines of the pool, the Purge's hideous head stretched up, a lopsided mouth opening beneath what could pass - in certain demonic circles - as a nose. It slammed against the stone wall, clutching at it with shifting limbs. Straining sounds rumbled from it as it lifted a portion of its ponderous bulk onto the stone ledge, water trailing off it like a grey cloak. Meris stood, surveying the shadow haunted hall for a route of escape.

From the pool the creature's voice rang again, calling her name, trying to lure her to it. It was acting strangely – well, stranger than usual for a monster made of sentient poison and hate. It shook and shuddered in the water, arms and the occasional leg shivering when they broke the surface and clawed at the stone. It reached out towards her, scratching at the tiles.

She watched as the nearest limb, an ungodly fusion of reptilian talon and lobster claw, collapsed into a streak of nightmare-themed mush with a soft wet slap. Said horrible mush splattered across the stone, growing into half formed crustaceans and insects that limped towards her before dissolving into lifeless, grey stains.

The destruction of that over-reaching limb was not a singular occurrence. Two others followed suit, and a fourth would have followed if the creature had not retracted it prematurely. The Purge roared as it churned in the water, shifting back and forth like a caged animal.

Meris took a first cautious step forward as realisation dawned... that is *exactly* what it was. A slightly less cautious second step followed.

"You can't leave the water!" She called to it, the merest hint of a smile on her lips. "For all that you are, you were never designed to be able to leave the Network!" She rose on the balls of her feet to get a better look at the monster within the pool, making sure to remain out of reach of the remaining tendrils that swiped at her desperately.

The Purge said nothing, brooding and hissing in its aquatic kingdom. Meris struggled to contain a small giggle of glee, a harmonious and long forgotten sound.

"After all that you have done, all those you have killed to get to me, you are stopped by your own limitations!" Meris skipped backwards and span in place, her vibrant green tunic swirling around her in the gloom. "I'm free of you, monster; you have failed. There is one Meris left, and she is going to find the light."

She turned her back on the creature that frothed and raged in its prison, howling her name.

It assaulted the wall, cursing as it tried to crawl after

her. Meris smiled, the once dread voice now impotent. The hall opened up before her, lit dimly by blue lights that danced in the distance. Her skin shone amongst the shadows, her body healing and strengthening itself as she walked lightly across the black marble stones.

At last she was safe, and soon, she would be free.

It was a shame, then, that a gunshot had to go and spoil everything.

DATA TRANSCRIBED FROM THE VIDI-LOG OF:
Captain Horatio Scara

DATA RETRIEVED FROM [CLASSIFIED], STATUS:
NON-OPERATIONAL

DATA RETRIEVAL DATE: [CLASSIFIED]

I believe I am going mad.

I cannot sleep, Her eyes haunt my dreams; their guns rouse me from them.

—::—

I have made contact with our new arrivals.

The Mother's Men follow two brothers, twins by the look of it. I have instructed them to leave this place, or die attempting to take it. They have accepted the latter part of my offer, and have spent the last few days ineffectually assaulting the Institute.

"Give us your god!" seems to be their favourite war chant; if only they knew how far from grace we were.

The Mother's Men have been smart enough to bring artillery. Despite having some impressive bark, it is severely lacking in bite and the resulting damage we have sustained so far is purely cosmetic.

They do not trouble me; there's no chance of them getting in here.

—::—

Progress on cloning the subject has gone poorly.

Whereas before the subjects were wild, uncontrollable creatures of great strength, the new tests produce nothing but embryonic failures, kept barely alive by the MERIS program held within them.

The constant failure is taking its toll on Porvine; I am becoming concerned for him.

I have refused his team access to the Purge. On their request, the security corps have instead taken responsibility of disposing of the subjects.

After seeing the toll it has taken upon my men, I am now conducting the task personally.

Their faces torture me. I see them reflected in the propaganda that covers our walls, their eyes accuse me. I will order the images removed.

I can feel their blood on my hands. I believe I am going mad.

I have seen little of Bos these last few nights; she has been consumed by her work. I have debated speaking to her of my concerns, though I fear it may undermine me.

I believe I am going mad.

They've started shooting again.

Chapter Twelve

THE bullet struck the tile next to her, cracking a white spider's web across the dark surface. Meris shrieked, recoiling from the point of impact. Two more shots were fired, one whizzing over head and the second skittering off into the darkness.

Rough voices broke into the hall, whooping and cheering. Firelight bounded in ahead of them, racing down one of the wide staircases that curled beside the statue. The orange glow licked the jubilant faces of a small posse of Reds, one of whom was hastily thumbing cartridges into one of those ugly-looking rifles.

There were four of them in total, including the bloke with the rifle. "She's here, we've got her!" barked the closest, a young woman with a shock of hair dyed pillar box red to match her ragtag uniform. "Crubben, get on the blower to Base and let them know we've got her!"

A portly chap, damp of face and fair of hair nodded, racing back up the stairs and through a pair of mahogany doors. Meris's face was a picture of animal terror as they approached. She took a few startled steps backward, retreating into the darkness.

"Stay where you are!" The woman commanded, drawing a grim-looking dagger from the battered leather sheath that hung from her hip, "Oh, you stay right there, doll." Her left eye shone hungrily from amid a thick smear of kohl, the right obscured from view by a smattered fringe. "Ghertski, you got her covered? I don't want her getting away again."

"Oh, I got her, Bos." The thug with the rifle eyed her through the sights, resting the gun on the balustrade that ran beside one of tumbling waterfalls. His tongue poked out beneath a mousey moustache. "She moves an inch and *blam*, right between those pretty little brows of hers."

"Well, just make sure your trigger finger is steady. I don't want you painting this place with her brains just yet." She smiled at Meris as she spoke, her single visible eye flaring with deranged desire.

"Oh yes. We've got a lot planned for you, freak, a *lot* planned. Drastor, grab her and let's get out of here. This place is like a fucking tomb." Bos shivered slightly and turned to where Drastor, a big burly chap with a tattoo of a rat on his neck, stood staring into the pool.

Drastor was distracted. "'Ere Bos, that horrible black thing is in here. It's... well, it's acting weird. It's doing something."

The Purge had remained quiet since the arrival of its masters, seething just below the surface. It moved now, sliding forwards with renewed purpose. That foul head rose from beneath the waves, spitting claws and popping eyes across its gelatinous form. Its maw opened wide as a flurry of tentacles surged towards the watching militant.

Bos cried in surprise as it engulfed Drastor, knocking the big man backwards before dragging him beneath the waves.

"Ghertski, shoot it! Fucking shoot it!" The bloke with the 'tache got off a few rounds, his gun rattling bullets ineffectually. The Purge drank the hot lead with glee. A writhing pustule detached itself from the main mass that feasted upon the fallen Drastor and slithered across the surface of the water. The redheaded woman could do nothing as it raced up the waterfall and leapt through the spray to land upon the helpless Ghertski. The man's gloved hands went to his face as the black mass wrapped around him, the brief struggle quickly ending as he tumbled over the barrier.

The crack of meat and bone striking rock was astonishingly loud, and echoed for a surprisingly long time.

The Purge reformed, a single massive monster split by a deep mouth. It bellowed victoriously as it rose like a terrible kraken from the frothing brine. Two fat tentacles, dripping with eyes and teeth and humanlike fingers, whipped out into the hall. The first coiled backwards and grabbed the crumpled corpse of Ghertski from where he lay, broken across the rocks. The tentacle lifted him high into the air before casually tossing him into its wide, slobbering mouth. There was a sickening crunch as it chewed, its mouth opening wide to reveal blocks and blades of yellow teeth stained by blood and gore.

Bos turned to run, ignoring Meris, who watched in horror as her captors were slaughtered.

The Purge reached out to her, splitting its coiling limb into a writhing net of thrashing tendrils. The fleeing woman slashed at the tentacle as it leapt around her, her knife cutting through the oily substance with ease. It fell, flopping madly on the marble before collapsing, only to be replaced by two, three, four more that pressed around her.

She cried and swore with exertion as she hacked at them, the blade of the knife slicing through the air, flashing in frenzied arcs. It was a respectable effort, but one that was ultimately doomed.

A web of tentacles captured her, crushing her arms to her sides and lifting her from her feet. Blood dripped from where claws and spines pierced her skin, squeezing a strangled scream from her throat. Meris could only watch from the shadows as vicious mouths opened along its sides, ready to receive the woman that was drawn towards the pool.

"Mine," the Purge rumbled, "the Meris is *mine*. You are *mine*."

Bos's struggling cries were cut short as her head was dragged beneath the churning water. Below the waves the Purge held the struggling woman firm within its coils of black anti-flesh. Air fled in glittering bubbles from her mouth and nose as it collapsed her ribcage, crushing her lungs. Bos's vision darkened as it wrapped around her. The Purge's tentacles plunged deep into her nostrils, filling her mouth with black filth that swelled her throat and bloated her body. The creature snarled laughter at her, its burning red eyes searing through her mind.

The Purge's attack had lasted mere seconds, and now Meris stood alone.

The water in the pool frothed and boiled, releasing all manner of noxious maladies into the air. She thought she could hear a faint scream, a terrified pleading on the edge of hearing that slowly died beneath the sound of churning water. Behind her the hall opened up like a void, flanked by offices and balconies half-lit by the clustering blue lights.

"Meris..." her name, twisted and warped, echoed once more through the hall.

Something pale slapped wetly onto the stone wall. A human hand. It twitched, the fingers bending in unnatural positions. Despite herself, curiosity moved her, her feet making pitter-patter sounds on the black marble. She held her breath.

A second hand escaped the murky depths and grasped at the stone, the broken nails scratching at the granite. The water rippled as a bowed head, covered in bright red hair that was slicked to the skull, rose from the surface.

The girl watched as Bos pulled herself wearily from the pool. She sank to her knees, hands splaying out before her. Meris stepped backwards, a shiver going through her as the woman coughed thickly. Black ink poured from her convulsing throat, splashing across her fingers. She cried aloud, her shoulders shaking as the flow of black bile slowed. It seeped across the tiles; steam rising from it, carrying its foul smell towards the vaulted heavens.

Her clothes were tattered and torn, the exposed skin swollen and unnatural, like that of a drowned thing. Her head remained bowed, her hair clinging in wet ropes across her shoulders. "Merisss," she wheezed, bringing forth another gout of black slime.

Meris' hands flew to her lips as Bos looked up, her eyes pupiless orbs of terrible red. She smiled, her face splitting as sharpened fangs tore her cheeks, carving a vicious path through the lifeless flesh.

The Purge cackled behind the dead eyes, forcing its puppet to stand. Red fabric hung from the walking corpse in tatters, trailing along the wall like the broken wings of some great insect. Black claws and snickering maws pushed through her skin, bristling across her arms and legs as it stepped down onto the marble.

"You are mine." It hissed.

The creature strode across the room, the broken bones in its stolen body giving it an awkward and disjointed gait. It moved in a celluloid fashion, twitching from one position to another, flitting between leering pools of shadow.

Meris ran, but had barely taken a few steps before it was upon her.

Iron hard fingers closed about her throat. She gasped

as she was lifted from her feet, the red eyes burning into her. Her hands flew to the thing's wrists, her legs kicking out in desperation as it crushed the life from her body. She tried to shift in its grip, but to no avail; once again the Purge's very touch drained the energy from her, paralyzing the girl, trapping in a single form.

The corpse grinned, black filth dripping from its mouth to splatter across dead flesh.

"At last, little sister," it hissed, Bos's voice twisted in mockery, "you are mine."

The world shrank around her, darkness eating away at everything beyond those burning eyes.

The hall became a grey tableau in which she was locked, face to face, with her not-quite-so-mortal enemy. She could feel the calluses on the dead woman's fingers dragging against her skin as they squeezed harder. The Purge unleashed itself in full, the physical assault on her person paling in comparison to the attack on her mind. Its will tore into her with a greater ferocity than ever before, consuming her thoughts and ravaging her soul.

This time, there would be no way out for her. There was no shining knight; no piscine protector to save her, nor any distraction to stall its grim duty. In its grip she died as it drew her from herself, draining everything she was to sate impossible hunger. Its eyes rolled in ecstasy, the burning glare showing through broken bone and stretched skin.

It didn't taunt her now; it didn't need to. It merely laughed.

It laughed, and laughed, and laughed.

The sound rolled off of the distant walls, echoing back like sinister applause. Meris' vision blurred, nausea bubbling through her as the abomination drank deep from the living energy that she encapsulated. Those precious golden motes that held her, that carried her mind and allowed her to take a thousand forms, to heal and to grow and to help, were drawn out through her skin, their passage marked by golden pathways that lingered on her body.

They moved unnaturally as they left her; a fusion of high chemistry and eldritch arts that waltzed through the air, heedless of gravity.

The Purge sucked them in, taking deep breaths between bouts of laughter as they were absorbed into its putrid body. Watercolour strokes of ash tainted Meris's body as the life was drained from her. Her limbs twitched feebly in its inescapable grasp.

In her mind she walked alone through endless grey corridors lit by cold fire as her sanctuary burned. The Purge would consume all she was; it had already penetrated further than her earlier defences would have allowed. Little by little, all that she was fell away, tumbling into the void to be devoured. That harsh laughter filled her ears, shaking the foundations of her very soul. She could taste its acrid hatred on her tongue. Pain was now little more than an afterthought, an electric sting atop the crushing emptiness that closed about her. It had taken the ability to feel from her already.

The monster had won.

Any second now it would strike its final blow, tearing through the mental layers of her hive mind to pluck the very last blip of consciousness from her. It would take her, and then... and then what? Meris paused, the shade of a girl standing alone amidst the rubble and fire and smoke.

The Purge would strip her soul from her body, shattering her mind as she did so. What remained, if anything, would be nothing but dead pseudo-flesh.

And then what, exactly?

Despite the horror and pain of her consumption, the hell of which surrounded her, within this mental bower her thoughts were considerably coherent. Well, as coherent as one can be, given the above situation.

The question stood out, a queer point of logic nestled within the madness. *What would happen after she died?*

What would the Purge do, once it had completed its task of executing her? Her thoughts turned to the fish that remained within the system, those that had so far escaped the Purge's savage butchery. They swam about her now, threading from her memories to dance as rainbows around her.

Her life was over; this was a given. Around her, the cracks of her sanity spread like fireworks, a final celebration of her being before it was lost forever. With her dead, would it stop? She thought this unlikely. Still, once full, what would become of a creature driven by hunger? Was it her life, now, that sustained it?

The life she clung onto was won by fear and sacrifice. She ran and hid, while death fell upon those around her. Now she was alone, there was no one to save her, and no one to die in her place.

No one but her. The choice was clear.

Had the Purge turned its attention away from its gluttonous gorging for but a second, the burning embers that sat in the puppet's eye sockets would have noticed the grey smile that fell upon Meris's dying lips.

For the final time in her short life the girl launched a mental assault, focusing the entirety of her multifaceted mind into a single movement. This time, however, she held nothing back. She burned away fear, denied herself consequence. The Portrait's eyes were upon her now, those terrible points of violet staring out into the world. She drew them to her, focusing on every aspect of her. She pulled memories from every form; from Scara, from the Great Gollollopp, from every fish and plant and human she had encountered.

They wove around her, her consciousness soaring free of her sanctum of sentience on wings of golden fire. Her muscles surged forwards, her entire body pulling together in a single desperate motion.

The Purge filled the world, its billion eyes glaring at her with amusement. She dove forward, entering its mind and drawing out every sick vision it held within. She shone like a supernova amid the blackness of its soul.

"What now, little sister?" its voice echoed, "Now you come to me? Now you seek to know me, as I know you? So be it."

Its laughter rang like thunder, drowning her reply. "So be it." she whispered.

In the hall her arms struck out, her hands clamping around the Purge's hominid skull. It screamed in surprise, jerking backwards. Meris's thumbs found its eyes, her skin blistering as she punctured the smouldering orbs. She shrugged off the pain; burnt thumbs are nothing when your very existence is being torn apart atom by atom.

The Purge released its grip, sagging forwards as she clung to it. Her veins glowed golden, thick pulses of light throbbing beneath the mottled grey of her skin. They erupted from her like miniature solar flares, flowing in beaded lines down and into the Purge's drooling maw.

Meris drove at its mind, flooding it with everything she had, lighting the darkness.

The laughter grew louder as she burned in its grasp, the primal urge to consume blinding it to any sense of self-preservation. "Yes!" it howled with sick glee, "Yes! Come to me, sister, come to me!" Meris screamed as it devoured her, unable to form neither thoughts nor words as it feasted upon her.

Unseen wind tore at her hair, her body wracking as the life was siphoned from her.

Her mouth went dry, her mind devoid of anything other than darkness and pain. Yet still she clung to it, squeezing its grimacing face with the last vestiges of her strength. Its tongue flopped heavily from its mouth, the thick tubular muscle lapping hungrily at her as its arms shivered and flailed like twisted branches amid a tempest. A vicious claw ripped through her upper arm, sundering dry flesh and teasing a few straggling drops of saffron blood out into the air.

As one, they sank to their knees, the girl fading as the laughter increased. Golden flecks frothed on its face, shimmering like starlight atop the sludge that seeped from its mouth. The girl screamed. It was all that she had left. She screamed, though her lungs had long since collapsed, her heart long since ceased to beat. Her eyes perceived nothing, only darkness, the cold abyss that separates life from death.

Therefore, she didn't see the trickling black filth that spilled from its lips run bright with molten gold. She didn't hear the Purge begin to choke, nor feel its body convulse as it scratched desperately at the marble floor, talons snapping as it dug grey grooves in the unsympathetic stone.

It coughed out a desperate protest, the words drowning in the living light that cascaded between its fangs. The dying light of the girl filled it, swelled it.

"No!" it gargled, striking out, raking and battering her body with its claws while its feet shuddered against the marble, "No. It is too much! It is, it is- sister..."

The wounds it inflicted upon her went unnoticed as the sea of golden fire stripped away Bos's flesh, its words dying in a hiss. The light seeped between her grey fingers as it immolated the anti-flesh that howled within the skull. Sulphurous steam cloaked her, venting in bulbous clouds from the creature whose screams now rose above her own. The girl fell heavily onto her elbows as the hated enemy withered and writhed in her grasp.

Where living evil had once ridden upon dead flesh, nothing remained but bleached white bone that broke upon the floor. The Purge's voice dwindled into nothing, the red glare fading, until silence fell. Alone, Meris hugged the skull to her breast, its polished surface glistening eerily in the faint blue light.

"Sacrifice." the whispered word fell from her cold lips as she toppled sideways into the dust.

The skull slipped free from her grasp, clattering loudly as it bounced across the hall before spinning to a halt.

This may be my final entry.

She speaks to me.

The Mother's Men breached our lower defences almost five nights ago, and all service levels are now in Red hands. Our reports claim a maintenance bay in Segment Gamma was left unsealed, un-barricaded.

Segment Gamma was lost in the first hour; our chief engineer, her prime team of technicians and their auxiliaries, H division, eight SyMons and almost two hundred civilian staff along with it.

Segment Echo fell within a day: two tech teams, R, Q, P and most of division C, three SyMons and over seventy civilian staff. Deceased.

We retreated from Segment Delta this morning; the reports of our losses are still coming in.

We have been betrayed.

—::—

The sealing of that entire district was overseen by Bos personally; I have her signature in my hand.

The traitor must have been one of her own. Only a member of her tech team could have overridden those locks, and disabled the charges without being detected.

Bos McClusky, Chief Engineer, Paragon Class: Missing, presumed captured or deceased.

I can almost taste the smoke from here. I hope she gave them hell.

—::—

We have blockaded the main gateways to what Segments remain, and I have sent men loaded with blast charges to collapse the service corridors.

We'll seal them in there.

Whatever treachery the snake in our midst has set will go no further, I'll lose no more to the work of turncoats.

My men are on high alert; those closest to me know we have been betrayed. It is my hope that the bastard died in the fall of Gamma, if only for his sake.

—::—

Our progress on the MERIS project has all but failed.

The last batch, the one we had weighted all of our hopes upon, were barely alive.

I can no longer bring myself terminate these failures myself.

The grim duty returned to Porvine and his team.

In hindsight, I believe that is what drove him to do it.

Cornum Porvine, Chief Science Officer of the Institute: Deceased.

Suicide, poison, he and his valet both.

They were discovered in the early hours of this morning, in his chambers. I have ordered the bodies covered, the room sealed. News of Porvine's death has been a hammer blow to the effort. What little morale the Science Corps had left has been shattered.

As Commanding Officer, I have instructed that their work be continued. By maintaining a purpose they have something to fight for. They will still have hope.

And perhaps, if I have the work continued, She will stop calling to me.

—::—

I cannot sleep, Her eyes haunt me.

I believe I am going mad.

What systems can be automated shall be made so, and left to run in isolation. Who knows, maybe we'll get lucky and, after all this, it will be a machine, a computer following a program, that creates the Saviour of Earth.

Part of me likes the idea of that.

We will fall back to the Citadel. All hands have been drafted into moving the machines necessary to continue the work. The work must continue.

I believe.

Chapter Thirteen

SYMON rubbed his piston-powered hands across the dual cameras that were his eyes, aping a human expression of disbelief that he had retained somewhere deep within his memory banks. The action served only to cover the lenses in a fine layer of grease that had to be hastily and fussily wiped away with a pale green rag produced from a small compartment in his shoulder.

The grainy image on the circular screen before him returned, the brilliant flash of light receding until a single human-shaped filament burned weakly amongst the darkness. It glowed, smouldering amongst the dust before winking out, leaving nothing but ash.

SyMon made a startled sound that hung in his electronic throat for quite some time. In the hall's vaulted ceiling surveillance cameras whirred in their cradles, rocking back and forth as they strained to get a better view. Elsewhere, their kin tracked the movement of humans - not very *nice* humans - as they raced to the main hall.

SyMon tried not to panic. SyMon failed.

The MERIS was in trouble, and the Ophanim were only at eighty-six percent. He jabbed at the flickering blue bars that crept up the hissing display with the urgency of a procrastinating mollusc.

What to do, what to do?

He had tried to rouse Tamik, but the young man was dead to the world. *He must be very tired indeed,* reasoned the robot.

Alone, and with full responsibility falling squarely upon his skinny, metal shoulders, SyMon turned his full attention to rousing the Institute's long neglected systems. The first set of audio had failed to play, leaving only dust to fall from the speakers that hung in almost every room of the complex.

It was not a good sign.

SyMon began to worry, his click-clacking fingers wringing together as he trundled from screen to screen.

There was movement in the hall; several shadows approached the grey smudge that was all the cameras could detect of the fallen MERIS. This did nothing to settle SyMon's nerves. Oh, how he wished Tamik would wake up! The current situation was far beyond his remit and required human intervention, he was sure.

There was a flourish of blue pixels across a nearby screen, as the number eighty-eight metamorphosed into an eighty-nine. SyMon jabbed at it irritably, and resumed his impotent vigil as the shadows gathered around the fallen girl.

–::–

Lott trudged through the gloom, his iron-capped boots thudding loudly. "Fan out, you fucks!" he snarled at the posse of crimson clad lackeys that clustered nervously behind him. "What are you afraid of? It's half-dead already." The grumbling grunts did as they were told, moving across the hall in dribs and drabs. Guns and blades were thrust into shadows, nozzles curling around the columns in search of hidden foes. More than one muzzle flashed as bullets were fired at bogeymen and reflections.

Lott scowled at them.

Recruit Crubben sweated next to him, panting as he jogged to keep pace with the striding brute. Lott scowled at him, too.

As he neared his quarry he ceased, for now, his scowling. Instead his eyeballs took to glaring, straining in his hairless head at the tiny bundle of otherworldly fabric that lay before him. He tightened his grip on that horrible rifle of his, the sweat on his mitts lifting black grease from its surface.

He stopped several paces from where Meris's lifeless body lay. Lott turned to Crubben. "Go and check it out." He barked, prodding the damp chap with his rifle. Motivation and delegation, he nodded proudly to himself, were both signs of good leadership.

Crubben looked at him mournfully, and raised a reedy sound of protest. Lott took his comments on board, and prodded him harder, "Get on with it!" he growled. The man scuttled forward, his feet padding on the floor while his over-sized uniform whipped around his ankles. His scuttling slowed to a shuffle, and ended up as a cautious creep as he drew near, and then nearer still.

Meris lay on her side, her back to the meek marauder. Her arms spilled out above her head, pale and wraithlike against the expanse of her hair, now dulled to a green as dark as deep water.

Crubben dithered above her, his eyebrows quaking. Sweat pooled about his baggy eyes and clung to his top lip, "Err, hello?" he called in a pathetic sort of way.

"Don't fucking *talk* to it!" roared Lott, from a safe distance. He waved his rifle irritably.

Crubben flapped, exasperated, "Well, what am I supposed to do?"

"I don't fucking know." Lott was losing control of the situation here. "Poke it or something." he suggested forcefully.

Crubben flapped again, looking hither and thither for something to do the suggested jabbing with. His brief and stationary search produced nothing other than a shrug. "Poke it with what?"

Lott's frustrated groan was joined, albeit weakly, by one spilled from Meris's lips.

Crubben made a craven sound, jumping out of the way with surprising grace. One could almost detect a hint of pirouette. Lott snatched up his rifle from where it hung about his neck and levelled it at the stirring girl. The heads of the Reds turned, and all eyes fell upon her.

There were clicks and chur-chicks as a motley medley of grim looking guns were swung in her direction. Those that lacked such firearms waggled cudgels, bludgeons, truncheons and other similar-sounding things with menace.

Meris slowly rose into a sitting position, her grey limbs moving autonomously. A golden light shone weakly in her breast, pulsing with every heartbeat. It traced through her veins, rippling beneath her skin like sleeping lightning. Her eyes swung about the room, causing the crowd to step back as her gaze turned to them. She stood weakly and stepped forwards, her feet settling like butterflies upon the cold stone.

Sweat beaded on Lott's rosy head, shimmering on his furrowed brow. His crew waited on his command as she walked towards him. Her eyes stared sightlessly; two orbs the colour of a harvest moon that spilled a haunting half-light into the gloom.

Lott gripped his rifle with added force, threatening to crush the lower grip in his mighty mitt. His jaw locked. Down the sights a cross hair twitched across the otherworldly girl's forehead. Lott fought to keep it steady, desperate not to show any sign of fear before his subordinates.

He took a half-step backwards, a reluctant creep. Cold sweat dripped down his spine as she raised a hand towards him. "Stop, you just fuckin' stop right there!" he roared, rather too loudly. There was a slight squeak beneath his words and he dared any of his men to notice it. "I mean it! You'd better fuckin' stop, right now."

The calloused skin beneath his trigger finger itched across the warm metal, feeling every pit and prickle in the rough surface. She glided across the floor, time slowing around her as she reached out in mimic of the statue of serenity that loomed behind her. He could feel the nervousness of his ragtag war band as they shuffled in their boots, their weapons following her path across the marble.

His breath was tinny; he could taste it on his tongue. Her lips were closed; those warm, pale eyes unblinking. There was a small crunch of boot on dry bone as he took the other half of that step backwards.

He jabbed the gun forwards, "I said fuckin' stop, stop there!" His voice cracked out like a gunshot.

"Oh, Brother!" Latt's voice shattered the moment. He growled in a sing-song sort of way, as he leaned over one of the wide balconies that stood on either side of the hall. "What in the name of fetid fuck is going on here?"

He gripped the brass railing, his arms shaking with that constant and low-level rage he wore like a favourite dressing gown. The remainder of the Red invasion force had arrived with him, and now marched down a trio of sweeping staircases to bolster the ranks below.

Lott lowered his weapon, scuffing his shoe across the floor. "Well, we found her- it. We found it." The MERIS paused, her head twitching sightlessly towards the source of the new sound.

Latt's beardy face was split by a dangerous grin. "I

can see that brother, I can fuckin' see that," he hissed, "So why the fuck is it still alive?" A crowd of crimson filled the hall, shifting in the shadows. Lott felt their eyes prickle across him, niggling at his skin as his authority evaporated. The MERIS stood in silence, her dark hair lifting in the breeze. In the expectant void Lott felt as if he could almost hear the surges of light pulsing through her... it.

He shrugged, "We were about to-"

"No, no, fuckety no." Latt cut him off, slamming his hand on the railing, causing it to clang out across the hall. "Did you forget why we are here? What the whole point of bringing this place down was? After all this time, after all we've won and lost? Has it slipped that tiny mind of yours?"

The abashed Lott glowed scarlet, "No." he mumbled.

"Well, you could have fuckin' fooled me!" Latt reeled, flecks of spittle settling on his bristling beard. Part of it smoked slightly, the singed hair a scar of some recent tussle. "Can you imagine my surprise then, when I find you and your little squad of mates playing 'point the bloody pistol' around the main reason we are here at all? Maybe you'd like to invite it back to our old Ma's, for a nice cuppa and a fucking *biscuit*?"

Lott said nothing. Impotent fury shook his shoulders. The stares of the troops burned him. A hushed chuckle sounded somewhere in the shadows, a quiet mocking murmur that rippled here and there. His rifle had been released, and hung heavily from the strap across his barrel-thick chest. His fists were wrecking balls, coiled tightly around a squelching pocket of embarrassed sweat.

The bearded brother raised an eyebrow, "No? Ok then! Maybe we should do the job we're here to do, and kill the fuckin' thing, capiche?"

Lott continued to say nothing. Under the scrutiny of a hundred pairs of watching eyes, he took up his rifle; it was heavier than usual in his arms, and once again traced the cross hairs across the MERIS's forehead. Some colour had returned to it, streaks of turquoise running through the deep green hair, a hint of warmth returning to the grey flesh. His finger found the trigger.

"Oh no, no, no," Latt laughed from his lofty position, "No brother, I think we've had enough of guns for one lifetime. This is our crowning moment; it needs to be done with style, with ceremony." He gestured to Scara's knife, which still hung from Lott's belt. "Let's do this right. Why don't you take old Scara's knife, yeah, take that and gut it?"

Lott withdrew the knife carefully, holding it reverently in his hands. Its silver surface supped the light that fell upon it, drawing it in amongst the curves and ridges. The hilt was heavy in his hand, smooth and solid. It trembled in his grip, as though reluctant to conduct the deed it was about to be turned to.

"When you're ready." Latt sneered, stretching his arms wide.

Lott nodded. He moved as if in a dream, his legs leaden. The sounds of the crowd pounded in his ears, their jeers and cheers warped and distant. The MERIS remained a statue of tranquillity. Those shining eyes stared fixed ahead as he approached, seemingly blind to the silver and red threat that stalked towards her.

Lott held the knife out before him, its tip quivering. He pulled his arm back, a brutish bicep bulging as he prepared to strike. He swallowed hard, the lump pulsing painfully down his dry throat, and dropped his hand to her shoulder.

The MERIS gasped as he made contact.

It convulsed, as if struck by a surge of electricity; its back arching and limbs shuddering. Lott's fingers contracted involuntarily as his skin met hers, clamping his fingers in place. An electric current ran up his arm causing his muscles to twitch and shift beneath his skin. Lott watched wide-eyed as it crackled from his fingertips to dance across the poised blade.

The gasp had become a high pitched scream, the shrill mechanical whistle of escaping steam. It rose into the darkness, hanging in the air with a physical presence. Its eyes locked onto him, the violet pupils bursting into life as colour returned to the creature.

She - it - was warm to the touch, fizzing with an unnatural energy.

Lott's grip was iron, his arm a firm and fixed weight upon her.

"Come on now brother, finish it!" Latt's greedy words rang through the hall, fighting for dominance over the pounding of blood in his ears. Lott grit his teeth harder than ever.

The MERIS, now aware of its surroundings, met his gaze with wide-eyed panic. Its violet eyes flicked from the knife and then back to him. It opened its mouth to speak, as Lott drove the vicious point of his brother's blade home.

DATA TRANSCRIBED FROM THE VIDI-LOG OF:
Captain Horatio Scara

DATA RETRIEVED FROM [CLASSIFIED], STATUS:
NON-OPERATIONAL

DATA RETRIEVAL DATE: [CLASSIFIED]

I am alive, though the Citadel has fallen.

It has become a contest between us, a grim game: which side can achieve the greatest loss of life?

The game changes hour by hour; right now, we are winning.

It will not last for long.

The halls are a battleground, we are scattered and our enemies stand in their hundreds. The air is getting stale; it tastes of blood and smoke.

There have been reports of progress, from isolated groups entrenched in fortified positions.

A batch woke in the east, but the lab fell to the Reds before an evaluation could take place. The north tower reported a subject that was almost sentient, though the system was too fried to support it.

A call from level 66 at around the same time reported an auto-turret had activated, only briefly, but long enough to reduce nearly an entire squadron of Reds to ash.

This is promising; maybe Bos was right?

If we can create the MERIS, this whole thing is over.

—::—

With each passing day Her voice grows stronger, in every second of sleep She speaks to me. She is blinding, brilliant, terrifying. I consumed the last of my alcohol stash some nights back. If I cannot quieten my sleep, then coffee and stimulants will keep me from it.

We are close, I know it.

I have ordered that the sensors be activated, that any SyMon remaining is set to searching the automated birthing chambers for any viable subject. We must find Her - She must find us.

I cannot remain here.

Word has it that the leaders of the Mother's Men have entered the Citadel, the brothers Latt and Lott. It's about time I did what I do best, what I have been aching to do from the start: I will meet them in battle.

I can almost hear Her as I speak. The MERIS, whatever She is, is close.

Before I go I will leave Her a message, an order as the Commander of this tomb. She must escape; She must find the light and go out into the world. God knows, they need it.

This is Commander Horatio Scara, signing off.

Chapter Fourteen

IN his distant and lofty chamber, SyMon watched with automated horror as the MERIS was surrounded.

The screens squeaked and chirruped like excited sparrows, zooming and switching between viewpoints to best display the goings-on far below. A large man stepped from the crowd, the same large man that had appeared after the hated Purge ceased to function. Despite the grey and grainy image, SyMon could clearly see the glint of the knife in his hand. The man paused.

SyMon swung his head from the screen and over to the display where those vital loading bars crept ever upwards. Ninety-nine percent. The number wavered for an eternity. The robot's metal fingers flew to a waiting keypad, eager to punch in those all important activation codes. The screen flickered, those impish blue pixels teasing the watching droid. "Czome Ozn!" he groaned, bobbing impatiently on his hydraulics.

One hundred percent. The bars on screen stood proud and full for a brief second before vanishing to make way for a solitary spoked wheel which span in the centre of the display. A vaguely female voice sang out electronically from a nearby speaker, "Ophanim Online."

Had SyMon an extra arm, another item to add to the growing list of required upgrades, he would have punched the air. His fingers moved in a blur as the relevant codes were entered. The word [ACTIVATE] flashed by for a split second, before cavorting off with arms leaden with authorisation codes and passwords.

SyMon leaned back; it was done.

Even now, he could just about hear the announcement being played across the vast, concrete expanse of the Institute. He trundled along his tracking, rocking and swaying, to where Tamik lay motionless. "Stzill Slzeeping." SyMon sighed aloud to the empty and forgotten room. There was a whirr from his hydraulics as he moved towards the deceased technician. Carefully he brushed a lock of dry hair from the young man's face. He regarded him for a while. "Slzeep wezll, Tamzik." SyMon patted his shoulder with gentle inhuman affection. There was another whirr as he retracted his pistons and prepared himself to return to hibernation mode.

There was frantic movement on the screens behind him, the speakers bleeding faint human cries of alarm.

SyMon settled into position as his systems began to shut down. His job was done, and now the Ophanim could take over. He took a last look at Tamik and smiled impossibly. The young man would wake up any minute now, and would reactivate him. He would be interested in making some upgrades, certainly. There was a sound like a fading 'pee-oooh' as the robot powered down, the two lights in his eyes winking out for what would be the last time.

–::–

Lott staggered as the ground shook beneath him. Music blared from hidden speakers while banks of spotlights flooded the vaulted hall with light. From a hidden public address system a voice spoke, a vaguely-female voice, as the fanfare of trumpets subsided.

"Ladies and gentlemen, and all variations thereof!" It sang as red-cloaked thugs cast their eyes upward towards the sound and downward to the quaking ground, many going cross-eyed in the process. "The Institute is proud to announce the completion of a fully functioning MERIS. The Institute would like to thank all staff and residents for their hard work and dedication over the last-" The voice changed briefly, as an improbably-lengthy number was read aloud, before changing back to that singsong, almost feminine voice, "-Years, and invite you to share in the coming celebrations that will be held for staff and residents across all levels. Please report to your supervisor or nearest chapel for further instruction. Praise and hallelujah." The voice switched off with a rolling click.

There was some panicked movement amongst the crowd of Reds as portions of the floor moved below them. A gun was discharged, a cry went out. People pushed and shoved with a general determination to move in no particular direction, but certainly *away* from where they currently jostled. Lott watched wide-eyed, with the MERIS struggling fruitlessly in his grasp as four great, square slabs of black marble rose from the floor. Smoke and steam - and people who were not quick enough to get out of the way - fell from them, their mechanical movement lit by pulsing blue light.

"Ladies and gentlemen, and all variations thereof!" the voice returned, cracking briefly, "Please be aware that the Institute will now be activating the Ophanim Defence Program, until such time as the MERIS has been secured. All staff and residents are advised to report any and all sightings of the MERIS to your supervisor, or nearest chapel, and await further instruction. All staff and residents are advised to ensure their identification chips are up-to-date before approaching the MERIS. Praise and hallelujah!"

Somethings moved beneath the rising stones; somethings very large, and almost humanoid. The stones ceased their upward movement with a heavy hiss, revealing four chambers hung with wires and lit by those ever present blue lights. Steam rolled in billowing clouds; obscuring the somethings, those very *large* somethings, from sight.

A mailed fist, the size of a medium-sized dog - for reference - closed about a steel support girder. The girder bent in its grasp, putting the willies up the watching horde. From his balcony a purple-faced Latt screamed at his minions, his words drowning in the sea of sound that washed over the hall.

They stepped out from their chambers in unison, ducking through the oval doorways, their towering metal bodies gleaming in the twilight. The ground shook once more beneath their clanking steps as they waded into the sea of Red. Their wide, domed heads turned as one; four single eyes burning with azure fire, glaring monoptically at the struggling MERIS and the man who held her.

They scanned the knife, they scanned the man both inside and out, they read the pheromones in the air and registered heartbeats. Wheels revved and span, cogs clicking and motors straining as they each lifted an arm as thick as an oak trunk, pointing with a powerful, pneumatic digit. Lott looked between them, the incriminating knife held firm in his hand.

"UNAUTHORISED PERSONNEL," The nearest one to him boomed in electrified monotone, its voice sounding like the purring of a giant kitten inside of a church bell, "UNHAND THE MERIS." They took a step forwards, moving unimpeded as the Reds retreated towards the perimeter.

Lott considered his options, and made what he deduced would be the best course of action. He was wrong. With a nimbleness one would not expect from someone with such bulk, he span behind the MERIS, drawing his forearm across her throat, the knife poised to strike into her temple.

Meris choked and struggled as the brute evolved his grip on her into an even more unpleasant position. The smell of sweat and fear pricked within her nostrils. "Back off! Fuckin' back off!" Her captor commanded in that same ugly way. She pushed against him, her muscles weak as her body slowly recovered from her recent death.

"Back off!" Lott roared again, dragging the MERIS in a circular dance as he tried to face all four of the pointing titans at once, "I'll do it. I'll kill her, back off!" The giants stood like mountains, twice the size of a man. They hummed in unison as their accusing arms lowered. Lights flashed within them as they communicated, messages pinging between the fearsome four, coordinating their next move.

"Right. Err, well yeah, good!" Lott fumbled, looking up towards his brother, who fumed upon the balcony.

"ASSAILANT," the one to the east addressed him, suppressing any human voice, "UNHAND THE MERIS."

Lott twisted towards it, fear fuelling an erratic and wildness of movement. He bared his teeth; "Fu-" was all he managed.

With lightning speed the metal giant behind him strode forwards. It moved as a blur, piston-powered legs covering the distance in a fraction of a second. Its balled fist moved in a fluid motion, the merciless steel scything through meat and bone. The upper half of the man called Lott exploded in a fanfare of gore; the speed of the punch superheating the flesh, causing it to burst into a puff of pink steam.

The titanic automaton pivoted. "UNHAND THE MERIS," It commanded what was left of the man. It scooped the girl up to its chest, kneeling over her as the ragged remains of Lott's corpse fell away. Gunfire exploded from all corners of the room; plinking harmlessly off its wide, plated back. "PROTECT THE MERIS!" it instructed its colossal cohorts.

Lott's blood soaked into Meris' tunic, slicking it to her body. It dripped from her skin, sticking in her hair, the metal taste of it sour on her tongue. The chassis of her protector rang around her as bullets struck its polished surface. A being of pure machine; neither man nor beast, it regarded her warmly as its body shielded her from the red's onslaught. A circle of blue was emblazoned across its chest; a spoked wheel, a badge of honour. She lifted her hand to it, her fingers brushing lightly across the flawless metal.

"Ophanim," she whispered, the name bubbling up from the depths, a relic of someone else's memory, "Ophanim." It purred curiously, the sound vibrating on frequencies designed to specifically to comfort and calm her.

Around them, all hell broke loose.

The Reds had totally lost it upon seeing the demise of their second-in-command, and unloaded every weapon they had at the mechanical quartet. From his vantage point, flanked by some of his best men and women, Latt fired round after terrible round of his hand-cannon at the robotic giant that shielded the MERIS.

He roared orders to those below, but as these were mostly monosyllabic variations of "Fire!" and "Shoot!" it was mostly for his own sake.

The Ophanim stood, impervious to the streams of bullets that slipped off their carapaces like grey rain. Their blue optical sensors swept the room, crossing back and forth across the hate-fuelled crowd like search lights. They purred to each other, flashing information on their opponents back and forth.

A suitable response was agreed upon. "PROTECT THE MERIS." They chanted the command as sophisticated weaponry slid from their chunky forearms. Glistening guns, trophies of electric artillery clicked into place, clustering atop each other to form a beautiful, ballistic bouquet. Their designers had certainly not scrimped on the electroplated chromium; the shine alone was enough to dazzle nearby foes.

Unfortunately for those foes, a light dazzle was not the response agreed upon by the avenging trio. As a single unit, they went about their grim business with the detachment one would expect from those of such robotic persuasion.

The crowd dissolved into a fog of blood and screams as they opened fire. Bullets the size of chicken's eggs leapt from spinning magazines to punch gaping holes in the surrounding army, exploding on contact to shred bone and flesh. Blue lasers whirred above the bullets' dull boomings, pew-pewing as they doled out rapid-fire death.

Meris clasped her hands to her ears, her eyes shut tight against the sounds and sights of the surrounding slaughter. Her protector was unsurprisingly unfazed by the extermination, humming happily to her as its companions continued their terrible task.

A spinning grenade, lovingly decorated with silver filigree, detonated on the balcony; reducing the Red's elite corps to a splash of elite corpses. The crowd had begun to flee to the shadows, the blue lasers tearing through them as they ran. Ballistic-tipped bullets and arching grenades followed them, illuminating the shadowy corridors down which they fled with jets of orange fire.

A very definite silence fell upon the hall as the last fleeing Red collapsed into the dust. Her body glowed briefly, the laser pulse burning through her quivering flesh, and then nothing. Flames crackled in the distance, eating at the very bones of the Institute.

The Ophanim's scanners swept across the corpse-filled hall, picking at the immobile bodies, searching for the faintest signs of life. "MERIS SECURED." The silver giants growled their cold confirmation into the empty hall.

Meris's protector stood, its shadow falling across her. Freed from its steel embrace, the girl rose unsteadily to her feet. The ground trembled as the Ophanim took a defensive stance around her, forming a protective diamond. Her protector regarded her, inclining its head. "YOU ARE THE MERIS," it declared.

The girl was exhausted, her body still trying to repair itself. "Yes." she nodded. The Ophanim nodded back to her as it searched its databanks for a command from on high, though found the controllers oddly quiet. Instead, it turned to the next highest authority. "WHAT ARE YOUR COMMANDS?" it boomed as the galvanised giants gathered about her expectantly.

Her muscles were a patchwork of pain, her bones aching as the fibres of her being knitted themselves together. Her mind swam with fatigue, her thoughts drowning in a sucking mire of weariness. Her eyes tracked the burning devastation before her, flowing across the semicircle of broken corpses. Something heavy collapsed in the distance, sending smoke pouring through a side door.

"Please," she asked in a small voice, "Ophanim, take me away. Take me away from here."

The steel sentinel nodded again. Its body whirred,

the arm lowering towards her. Meris clambered onto it, pulling her protesting body onto the obliging limb. The Ophanim straightened, conveying the girl into a comfortable position upon its plated shoulder.

Remaining in position, the four welded warriors marched forth in formation; proceeding towards the towering doors of the Institute. The vast portals reached high into the vaults, their tops lost amongst the shadowed ceiling. Two circular locks flanked the reinforced doors, and towards these two Ophanim made their way, clanking and whirring with robotic determination. Mighty mechanical mitts gripped the spherical locking mechanisms; eliciting rusty groans as they set to the task of opening the last barrier to the world beyond.

−::−

Latt's fingers twitched across the polished wood, slipping in the slick of blood that spread across it. He pushed a smouldering corpse off of him and coughed, the movement wracking him with pain. His ears still rang with the sound of the explosion, his vision knocked off-centre, the world around him reduced to a realm of muted greys. He found the strength to swear, choking out expletives with the last of his ragged breaths.

His knee moved, somehow, bunching up beneath him and pushing him up from where he lay prone upon the blood-soaked mahogany. Determination moved him, hatred fuelling his torn muscles. Through the decorative slats that lined the balcony he saw the creature climb upon the shoulders of one of those lethal machines, riding upon it in some twisted mockery of a triumph.

His hand found his gun; a single bullet remained. He bit his lip as pain rampaged through him, snapping at his flesh like a pack of feral dogs. His feet slipped on blood as he struggled into a standing position, leaning and heaving against the brass railing.

The hand cannon was levelled, Latt's eyes crossing and uncrossing as he focussed on the pale, retreating figure. The iron sights shook as he fought to keep his aim steady. He closed one eye, his tongue poking out between a mess of bloody, broken teeth. Carefully, he lined up the shot.

–::–

The doors opened reluctantly, groaning and creaking as the locks slid back after an age of impermeable diligence. The first ray of *real* sunlight fell across Meris's face, painting her with an intoxicating warmth that spread throughout her aching body. A breeze - *real wind* - spilled through the widening crack, tousling her hair. Flowers blossomed upon her, unconsciously called into being as she soaked in the weak rays of orange sunlight.

The two Ophanim that moved ahead left the wheel locks and man-robot-handled the doors, their replicated muscles bulging as they dragged the vast monoliths apart. Meris beamed.

She knew nothing of the world beyond, but there was no doubt that a world of light and air, in which sunlight spilled unfettered was certainly preferable to a concrete prison haunted by shadows and death.

Her protector strode forwards, bearing her to freedom. Part of her suspected a hint of robotic pride in the powerful machine. She leaned into the nape of its shoulder, her fingers delighting in the feeling of sun-warmed metal. Despite the fug of uncertainty that clouded her thoughts, Meris looked forward to walking across the living earth. Away from this place, her life would be her own, something to grow and flourish amongst the world of the living.

She smiled, an honest and eager smile; she would fulfil her promise to the jellies.

The gunshot filled the silent hall, chasing the shadows away with its brilliant and terrible flare. The gun jumped like a leaping salmon from Latt's weakened grasp, trailing oily smoke as it was cast into the darkness below.

The bullet was well away.

Blue lasers pinged around it as the Ophanim rounded, their electric cannons firing automatically towards the source of the sound. Time slowed around the rotating projectile as it cut a lethal tear through the still air.

Meris's protector's arm moved to shield her from the speeding slug, the vast wall of steel curling around her. It was a fraction of a second too late.

The spinning bullet gleamed as it punched into her shoulder blade, passing through her body to burst from her chest in a flourish of golden blood. A surprised and pained gasp moved among the falling droplets of blood, a gentle song that fluttered from her parted lips.

Three Ophanim stood in triangular formation, unleashing spitting streams of blue fire upon the shuddering balcony. Their arms shook with the recoil, their feet wide apart, their knees bent to absorb the force.

The man called Latt, the elder of two twins, Deputy Big Chief of the Mother's Men and established beard-wearer, was immolated well and truly. The lasers burned his flesh from the world, melting his bones and reducing the whole lot of him into nothing more than a lingering, swearing vapour that rolled through the air. The balcony collapsed in the onslaught, crashing from its support columns to bury the dead beneath burning rubble.

Meris's protector purred in alarm, its voice becoming a melancholic lowing sound, as her body fell limp across its arms. Its squadron ceased fire, their weapons lowering as the sound registered among them. They coalesced into a worried huddle, the still girl at their centre. A small light struggled within her, skipping about her supine form without direction. The blood was thick upon her chest, moving slowly across her skin to drip like honey onto the powerful arms that cradled her. It made a small, sad sound, the ticking of a tiny clock, as it splashed onto the metal.

The Ophanim stood as statues as the light faded, the desperate pulse of life growing smaller and thinner as it painted itself across her body. It flared once, twice, and failed, swallowed by the grey shadows that once again dominated the girl's slender form.

Her sentinels remained silent, their eyes winking and flashing as they scanned the tiny creature that lay between them. The sun moved in the sky, pulling a shroud of oranges and reds across the steel giants, shadows curling beneath them. Smoke hung thick in the stone rafters, blotting out the twinkling blue lights. The sound of feasting flames roared in the distance, growing ever louder as fire consumed the flesh of the Institute.

And so, lacking further instruction, it was some time before the gathered titans showed any sign of life.

The one that held her purred again, the sound as strange and alien as ever. Their heads moved in unison, sunlight flashing from their wide faces as they turned to the crack of yellow light that was smeared between the two reinforced doors. Two were dispatched with a sharp and definite sound. They trudged towards the doors; their movements weighted by - if they were to be so personified and ascribed human emotions - what could only be described as grief. The opening was widened, the doors screeching as they scraped across the marble, until two of the giants could walk abreast between them.

This they did, resuming their diamond formation. Far behind them, something large collapsed as the flames took hold. They paid the sound no heed as they stepped through the towering stone arch, and into the sun-drenched world beyond.

Chapter Fifteen: An Ending

A gentle breeze rustled the dry grass, lifting spectres of dust into little haboobs that cavorted beneath a mustard-hued sky. The sound of waves on a gravel beach whispered in the distance. Here and there artillery pieces lay discarded, the remains of long abandoned camps scattered around them.

An enclosing wall of graffiti-clad cinderblocks, some fifteen feet high, framed a pair of iron-plated gates that hung loose from their hinges. Heavy chains were slung lazily from them, trailing towards the rusted remains of two armoured automobiles. They squatted lopsided upon their axles, clusters of brown grass huddling about them like crowds of carrion birds. The links clinked as the wind nuzzled against them. Bullet wounds punctuated the scene, peppering the cars and leaving circular scars in the crumbling concrete.

Four figures stood nearby, their heads bowed. One of their order moved, a grey bundle held reverently in its weapon-clad arms. Dirty light glinted off it as it knelt, lowering the precious parcel to rest upon the cracked earth. An odd purring rose from it as it looked upon the small, sad face that lay amongst the lifeless blades of grass. The Ophanim reached out, caressing the heart-shaped face with a chromium-plated finger. The MERIS's violet eyes were closed, the majority of the golden blood cleaned away as best as they could manage. Its hair spilled about it, the deep turquoise having faded to a pale mint that flowed across the barren earth like a sheet of silk.

The Ophanim looked upon her for a minute that could just as easily have been an hour, or a week. It stood slowly, the pistons hissing and wheels whirring as it straightened. The automatons moved in unison; taking formation at each point of the compass to stand in eternal vigil over their fallen quarry. Behind them smoke continued to billow through the open doors, crawling across the windowless heights of the Institute.

The sun glowed in the sky, pushing its rays through the dense layer of milky fog that hung above the surrounding city's jagged remains. The unyielding wind rippled through the grass and still tugged at the hanging chains, their percussion orchestra the only sound in the otherwise still world.

Well, almost still.

Something small, something tiny, crept through the strands of mint-green hair. Its clawed feet clung to a landscape of cold, grey flesh as it stumbled across the MERIS's forehead. Compound eyes reflected tiny pricks of light from their black surface as the little head twitched back and forth. A coiled tongue slipped from its mouth and tasted the air. It crouched, allowing a light breeze to ruffle its yellow and black fur, and set its wings trembling with excitement. They were new and untested, lying like a transparent cloak across its back. It turned on the spot, its little legs plodding along as it enjoyed the warmth of the sun.

The little bee bathed in the rays for a moment before, with a flicker of its wings, humming lazily into the air. It was *almost* possible that a tiny speck of golden light glimmered in its breast, winking as it flew up and away towards the clouds.

Almost.

About the Author

JD Atkin is a botherer of words, a drinker of ale and an established wearer of tweed. Originally from the murky backwaters of rural Nottinghamshire he moved to the city in pursuit of fame, fortune and interesting Sunday afternoon conversations. He believes he has found at least one of them.

In his spare time he enjoys racing velociraptors around his floating sky palace, frolicking with comely sirens in glittering gin fountains and lying about what he does in his spare time.

Divine Nature is his first published novel and he sincerely hopes you enjoy it.

ENJOYED
THIS BOOK? WE'VE GOT LOTS MORE!

Britain's Next
BESTSELLER

DISCOVER NEW INDEPENDENT BOOKS & HELP AUTHORS GET A PUBLISHING DEAL.

DECIDE WHAT BOOKS WE PUBLISH NEXT & MAKE AN AUTHOR'S DREAM COME TRUE.

Visit **www.britainsnextbestseller.co.uk** to view book trailers, read book extracts, pre-order new titles and get exclusive Britain's Next Bestseller Supporter perks.

FOLLOW US:

 BNBSbooks @bnbsbooks bnbsbooks

BRITAINSNEXTBESTSELLER.CO.UK